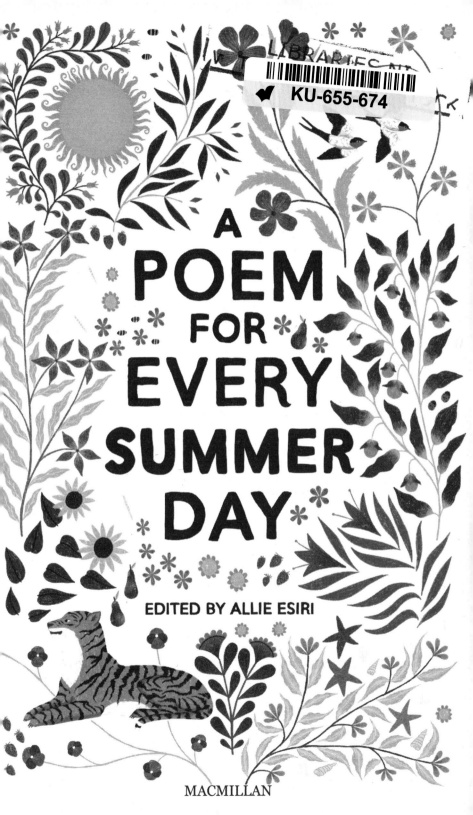

A POEM FOR EVERY SUMMER DAY

EDITED BY ALLIE ESIRI

KU-655-674

MACMILLAN

Published 2021 by Macmillan Children's Books
an imprint of Pan Macmillan
The Smithson, 6 Briset Street, London EC1M 5NR
EU representative: Macmillan Publishers Ireland Limited,
Mallard Lodge, Lansdowne Village, Dublin 4
Associated companies throughout the world
www.panmacmillan.com

ISBN 978-1-5290-4524-6

This collection copyright © Allie Esiri 2021
The permission acknowledgments on pages 300–302
constitute an extension of this copyright page.

The right of Allie Esiri to be identified as the editor
of this work has been asserted by her in accordance
with the Copyright, Designs and Patents Act 1988.

All rights reserved. No part of this publication may be reproduced,
stored in a retrieval system, or transmitted, in any form or by any means
(electronic, mechanical, photocopying, recording or otherwise),
without the prior written permission of the publisher.

Pan Macmillan does not have any control over, or any responsibility for,
any author or third-party websites referred to in or on this book.

1 3 5 7 9 8 6 4 2

A CIP catalogue record for this book is available from the British Library.

Printed and bound by CPI Group (UK) Ltd, Croydon CR0 4YY

This book is sold subject to the condition that it shall not,
by way of trade or otherwise, be lent, resold, hired out,
or otherwise circulated without the publisher's prior consent
in any form of binding or cover other than that in which
it is published and without a similar condition including this
condition being imposed on the subsequent purchaser.

For my parents

Contents

viii

July

x

August

Introduction

In this new anthology, the fourth in a four-part cycle of seasons, you will discover some of the most vibrant, bright and uplifting poems ever written about summer, and the most significant cultural events and historical anniversaries that lie in our calendars between 1 June and 31 August.

Summer is, of course, the season of heat (hopefully), holiday and hedonism; a time in which we're momentarily liberated from school and work and the weight of cold, dreary days and can go out and embrace nature. Our fondest summer rituals and memories will no doubt feature endless hours spent outdoors – in gardens, parks, fields, meadows, beaches, heaths, stoops and porches and anywhere else where we can bask in the sun's golden rays.

Luckily for us, the great poets never abandoned their practice during these months of leisure. Collectively they have given and continue to give us a near endless supply of beautiful, lucent summery poetry. It's a good thing, then, that this anthology offers you not just one, but actually two pieces of verse for each summer day, almost all of which have been drawn from my earlier curated anthologies: *A Poem for Every Day of the Year*, *A Poem for Every Night of the Year* and *Shakespeare for Every Day of the Year*. The hope is that the first daily dose will fill you with some hope and optimism to accompany those brilliantly cloudless summer mornings, while the second poem offers an opportunity to slow down after a long, humid day and lose yourself to an evening reverie – or a summer night's dream . . .

Within these pages you will find some of the most famous lines ever written about summer – such as the enchanting sylvan descriptions that give texture to Shakespeare's *A Midsummer Night's Dream.*

Among these diamonds of poetic fame, you will also discover an array of lesser-known gems that have served to capture the essence of the season in ways no less meaningful than the more frequently anthologised texts, all the way from the medieval exaltation 'Sumer is i-cumen in' to the contemporary performance poet Kae Tempest's meditation on their dog snoozing in the sun. Poems that celebrate the joys of summer are complemented by those by the likes of Mary Oliver and Mark Haddon which exhort us not to waste these warm days, nor overlook the everyday beauty that surrounds us. For writers such as Imtiaz Dharker and Carol Ann Duffy, meanwhile, summer brings with it bittersweet pangs of nostalgia for home and childhood pleasures.

Some of these poems make no direct reference to summer, but are featured here as they are imbued with the emotions and spirit of the season. For instance, Alfred Tennyson's 'Ulysses' is driven by a sense of adventure and boundless ambition, while John Keats's 'La Belle Dame Sans Merci' is as intoxicating as a hazy mid-July evening.

As ethereal as that Keats poem is, and other fantastical entries such as Matthew Arnold's 'The Forsaken Merman' and Elizabeth Bishop's 'Thunder' are, there are numerous pieces in this collection that emerge from momentous historical events, and times of all too real hardship. On 4 July, American Independence Day, you will encounter Walt Whitman's paean to his native USA, and ten days later you will be stirred by the French national anthem, 'La Marseillaise', on the anniversary of the national revolution that began with the storming of Paris's Bastille prison.

On 20 July we celebrate one of humanity's greatest achievements, the moon landings of 1969, with a poem by J. Patrick Lewis, and on the 28th we remember one of history's darkest chapters, the First World War, with Philip Larkin's devastating tribute to the loss of life, and innocence, suffered during the conflict.

Some events, such as the English Civil War, are brought to life by verse that transports us into the midst of the action, more real than an account in a history book. Meanwhile, a host of twentieth-century poems on the struggle for rights for minorities, women, and refugees by the likes of Maya Angelou and Charlotte Perkins Gilman offer us a sobering reminder that there is still work to do in the fight for equality. The unparalleled power of literature, after all, lies in its capacity to place us directly within the mind of another. A great poem invites us to see the world through the eyes of those whose experiences may otherwise be alien to ours and inspires us to bridge those gaps in understanding.

Variety is not only found in the subject matters and perspectives of the poems, but the very form of these texts. There are sonnets, ballads, odes, song lyrics, passages of blank verse, and rhyming couplets, as well as extracts from epics and snapshots from plays. Nothing is accidental in poetry, rather, as the Greek etymological root of the word reveals, it is a *made* thing. Each poem here has been crafted and honed to such a degree that every punctuation mark (or in the case of E. E. Cummings, lack thereof), every line break and rhyme helps the writer better express what to most of us remains inexpressible.

xvii

The short introductions at the start of each entry are there to offer up some key contextual information about that particular poem, writer or date; their intention is to illuminate.

The enduring wonder of poetry is that there is no set way to read it. You can choose to make it a daily habit, or opt to dip in and out. Maybe, just maybe, you'll find yourself seeking shelter from the beating sun one afternoon and devour the whole lot. However you decide to read this book, and whatever your favourite poem might be, I would love to hear from you.

Allie Esiri

June

1 June · Sumer is i-cumen in · Anon.

You don't have to be fluent in Middle English to grasp that this thirteenth-century medieval poem is a joyous celebration of the arrival of summer. In just a few lines we are transported to a balmy, bucolic scene in which seeds spring into bloom and a host of animals vociferously greet the arrival of warmer days. It would have been sung as a 'round' – which means at least three voices singing in unison, but beginning at different times. It has been set to music many times and is still popular today.

Sumer is i-cumen in,
Loude sing cuckow!
Groweth seed and bloweth meed
And spryngeth the wode now.
Syng cuckow!
Ewe bleteth after lamb,
Loweth after calve cow;
Bullock sterteth, bukke farteth, –
Myrie syng cuckow!
Cuckow! Cuckow!
Wel syngest thou cuckow:
Ne swik thou nevere now!
  Syng cuckow, now, syng cuckow!
  Syng cuckow, syng cuckow, now!

☾ **1 June** · Greensleeves · Anon.

On 1 June 1533 Anne Boleyn married Henry VIII – his second wife – and became queen of England. It is a popular notion that the song 'Greensleeves' was written around this time by Henry for his new wife. It became something of a hit, and by 1597 it was popular enough to be referenced in Shakespeare's *The Merry Wives of Windsor*. Anne's popularity with Henry, unfortunately, wasn't so enduring. Less than three years later he had her beheaded at the Tower of London.

Alas, my love, ye do me wrong,
　　To cast me off discourteously:
And I have lovèd you so long,
　　Delighting in your company!
Greensleeves was all my joy,
　　Greensleeves was my delight;
Greensleeves was my heart of gold,
　　And who but Lady Greensleeves.

I have been ready at your hand,
　　To grant whatever you would crave;
I have both wagèd life and land,
　　Your love and good-will for to have.
Greensleeves was all my joy,
　　Greensleeves was my delight;
Greensleeves was my heart of gold,
　　And who but Lady Greensleeves.

3

I bought thee kerchers to thy head,
    That were wrought fine and gallantly;
I kept thee both at board and bed,
    Which cost my purse well-favour'dly.
Greensleeves was all my joy,
    Greensleeves was my delight;
Greensleeves was my heart of gold,
    And who but Lady Greensleeves.

I bought thee petticoats of the best,
    The cloth so fine as it might be;
I gave thee jewels for thy chest,
    And all this cost I spent on thee.
Greensleeves was all my joy,
    Greensleeves was my delight;
Greensleeves was my heart of gold,
    And who but Lady Greensleeves.

Thy smock of silk, both fair and white,
    With gold embroider'd gorgeously;
Thy petticoat of sendal right,
    And these I bought thee gladly.
Greensleeves was all my joy,
    Greensleeves was my delight;
Greensleeves was my heart of gold,
    And who but Lady Greensleeves.

Thy girdle of the gold so red,
    With pearls bedeckèd sumptuously,
The like no other lasses had:
    And yet thou wouldst not love me!
Greensleeves was all my joy,
    Greensleeves was my delight;
Greensleeves was my heart of gold,
    And who but Lady Greensleeves.

Greensleeves, now farewell! adieu!
    God I pray to prosper thee!
For I am still thy lover true:
    Come once again and love me!
Greensleeves was all my joy,
    Greensleeves was my delight;
Greensleeves was my heart of gold,
    And who but Lady Greensleeves.

2 June • Bee! I'm Expecting You! • Emily Dickinson

Emily Dickinson's many short verses make use of a vast range of forms and perspectives. This little poem acts as a letter between two unexpected correspondents, wittily bringing the category of nature poetry into the world of human behaviour.

Bee! I'm expecting you!
Was saying Yesterday
To Somebody you know
That you were due –

The Frogs got Home last Week –
Are settled, and at work –
Birds, mostly back –
The Clover warm and thick –

You'll get my Letter by
The seventeenth; Reply
Or better, be with me –
Yours, Fly.

☾ 2 June · Summer · Christina Rossetti

Here Christina Rossetti uses the technique of listing to make a persuasive case for why summer, for her, beats all the other seasons.

> Winter is cold-hearted,
>   Spring is yea and nay,
> Autumn is a weathercock
>   Blown every way:
> Summer days for me
>   When every leaf is on its tree;
>
> When Robin's not a beggar,
>   And Jenny Wren's a bride,
> And larks hang singing, singing, singing,
>   Over the wheat-fields wide,
>   And anchored lilies ride,
> And the pendulum spider
>   Swings from side to side,
>
> And blue-black beetles transact business,
>   And gnats fly in a host,
> And furry caterpillars hasten
>   That no time be lost,
> And moths grow fat and thrive,
> And ladybirds arrive.

7

Before green apples blush,
  Before green nuts embrown,
Why, one day in the country
  Is worth a month in town;
  Is worth a day and a year
Of the dusty, musty, lag-last fashion
  That days drone elsewhere.

3 June • Joys of Ramzan • Sitara Khan

This poem details the rituals and customs observed during Ramzan. Ramzan is the Urdu name for Ramadan – the ninth month of the Islamic calendar, during which Muslims observe the tradition of fasting each day from dawn until sunset. Ramadan is intended to teach the values of patience and spirituality, and it is a time to focus on prayer and charity.

In Ramzan we please Allah,
We please Allah.
Offer Namaz and Jummah.

Shaitan is chained
Blessings gained
Vices forbidden
Sins forgiven.

Wings spread
Angels descend
Enfold us under
Realms of wonder:

They join us in daily routine
Rise early for Sehri cuisine
Five prayers and breaking the fast
Late to bed, midnight past.

In Ramzan we please Allah,
We please Allah.
Offer Namaz and Jummah.

To forget hunger,
We do Zikker, think of others:
Friends and neighbours.

Feasts are shared –
All our favourites: tikka masala
Spring rolls and potato phulkah

In Ramzan we please Allah,
We please Allah.
Offer Namaz and Jummah.

Good will ignites
Everyone unites
Invitations ring for breaking fast
Doors are opened to the outcast

We feel proud at having fasted
Made sacrifices, and having lasted
Made our lives a little harder
Seeking peace for the here and the hereafter

Radio voices, charity appeals,
Making gifts is no big deal.
Daddies empty their pockets
And hand over wallets
Mummies, their gold bracelets

Children caress their favourite toys
As they say goodbye for strangers' joys.
With bodies leaner,
the spirit's cleaner.

In caring, sharing we please Allah,
Please Allah
Offer Namaz and Jummah.

☾ **3 June** · Just One · Laura Mucha

In this poem, Laura Mucha uses a list and the repetition of the phrase 'one more' to illustrate just how many things the speaker of the poem enjoys.

One more mountain, just the one, one more trip away
  with Mum, one more apple rhubarb pie,
one more amber-lilac sky.

One more chocolate – plain and dark,
a peacock and a national park,
Arctic iceberg, Shetland sheep
and one more really good night's sleep. One more day of
  blazing heat,

one more friend I'd like to meet,
one more bike ride, one more hike, I'd talk to every bird
  and bee,
I'd soak them up, I'd set them free
with paint, with words, perhaps a song. Life is short and
  life is long,
so quickly please, before it's gone,

just one more poem.

On this day in 1913, Emily Davison threw herself under the king's horse at the Epsom Derby, dying four days later from her injuries. Davison was a key part of the suffragette movement, the group that demanded the vote for women. It remains unclear if Davison had meant to kill herself or if an attempt to bring attention to the movement had gone wrong, but either way she has gone down in history as a martyr for the paramount and fundamental cause of women's rights. The vote was given to women who met certain qualifications in 1918 – five years after the incident – but another whole decade would pass before women were given full voting rights in 1928. Charlotte Perkins Gilman, the writer of this poem, is best known for 'The Yellow Wallpaper' – a short story regarded as one of the most important feminist texts in the English language.

Because the time is ripe, the age is ready,
Because the world her woman's help demands,
Out of the long subjection and seclusion
Come to our field of warfare and confusion
The mother's heart and hands.

Long has she stood aside, endured and waited,
While man swung forward, toiling on alone;
Now, for the weary man, so long ill-mated,
Now, for the world for which she was created,
Comes woman to her own.

Not for herself! though sweet the air of freedom;
Not for herself, though dear the new-born power;
But for the child, who needs a nobler mother,
For the whole people, needing one another,
Comes woman to her hour.

☾ 4 June · Wiegenlied (Lullaby) · Anon.

In 1868 the German composer Johannes Brahms took the first verse of the famous Wiegenlied (a German word meaning 'lullaby') from a collection of German folk poetry, and set it to a gentle, rocking melody which is now instantly recognizable. Over 150 years later, exhausted parents around the world still rely on the Brahms Lullaby as an invaluable resource in the nightly ritual to get their children to sleep peacefully.

> Lullaby and good night,
> With roses bedight,
> With lilies o'er spread
> Is baby's wee bed.
> Lay thee down now and rest,
> May thy slumber be blessed.
>
> Lullaby and good night,
> Thy mother's delight,
> Bright angels beside
> My darling abide.
> They will guard thee at rest,
> Thou shalt wake on my breast.

5 June • Balloons • Sylvia Plath

The first public demonstration of a hot air balloon
by the French Montgolfier brothers took place on 4
and 5 June 1783 – for the first time men soared up
into the sky and saw the world from a completely new
perspective! The poet Sylvia Plath is known for heavy
and serious poems, but here both the writing as well as
the subject are lighter than air.

> Since Christmas they have lived with us,
> Guileless and clear,
> Oval soul-animals,
> Taking up half the space,
> Moving and rubbing on the silk
>
> Invisible air drifts,
> Giving a shriek and pop
> When attacked, then scooting to rest, barely
>   trembling.
> Yellow cathead, blue fish—
> Such queer moons we live with
>
> Instead of dead furniture!
> Straw mats, white walls
> And these traveling
> Globes of thin air, red, green,
> Delighting

The heart like wishes or free
Peacocks blessing
Old ground with a feather
Beaten in starry metals.
Your small

Brother is making
His balloon squeak like a cat.
Seeming to see
A funny pink world he might eat on the other side
    of it,
He bites,

Then sits
Back, fat jug
Contemplating a world clear as water.
A red
Shred in his little fist.

This short lullaby by the Elizabethan writer Thomas
Dekker was first published in 1603 – over 250 years
before Johannes Brahms composed his Wiegenlied.
Yet in spite of its early origins, Dekker's poem already
contains many of the phrases which we associate with
lullabies.

Golden slumbers kiss your eyes,
Smiles awake you when you rise;
Sleep, pretty wantons, do not cry,
And I will sing a lullaby:
Rock them, rock them, lullaby.

Care is heavy, therefore sleep you;
You are care, and care must keep you.
Sleep, pretty wantons, do not cry,
And I will sing a lullaby:
Rock them, rock them, lullaby.

6 June · Song of the Dying Gunner AA1 · Charles Causley

6 June 1944 was 'D-Day', the day of the Normandy landings during the Second World War. 160,000 British, American, and Canadian troops landed on the coast of Nazi-occupied France and fought their way up the beaches, in what is now remembered as the largest seaborne assault in history. An estimated 19,000 soldiers from both sides lost their lives on that one day.

Oh mother my mouth is full of stars
As cartridges in the tray
My blood is a twin-branched scarlet tree
And it runs all runs away.

Oh 'Cooks to the galley' is sounded off
And the lads are down in the mess
But I lie down by the forrard gun
With a bullet in my breast.

Don't send me a parcel at Christmas time
Of socks and nutty and wine
And don't depend on a long weekend
By the Great Western Railway line.

Farewell, Aggie Weston, the Barracks at Guz,
Hang my tiddley suit on the door
I'm sewn up neat in a canvas sheet,
And I shan't be home no more.

6 June · Cradle Song · William Blake

Most people are lucky to be blessed with either the gift of writing or of painting; the Romantic era polymath William Blake was a master of both. Continuing our run of lullabies, 'Cradle Song' is a wonderfully tender and affectionate poem that captures those all-too-rare stolen moments of calm in an infant's early years. Though the song may be used to soothe a baby to sleep, it is equally a poem for parents to cherish in the way that it describes their own innocent pride and love for their child. Its potential as a song was realized in 1938, when it was set to music by the great English composer Benjamin Britten.

Sleep, sleep, beauty bright,
Dreaming in the joys of night;
Sleep, sleep; in thy sleep
Little sorrows sit and weep.

Sweet babe, in thy face
Soft desires I can trace,
Secret joys and secret smiles,
Little pretty infant wiles.

As thy softest limbs I feel
Smiles as of the morning steal
O'er thy cheek, and o'er thy breast
Where thy little heart doth rest.

O the cunning wiles that creep
In thy little heart asleep!
When thy little heart doth wake,
Then the dreadful night shall break.

7 June · The Throstle · Alfred, Lord Tennyson

Summer is coming! Alfred Tennyson (ennobled as Lord Tennyson) remains the longest-serving Poet Laureate in history, occupying the role from 1850 to his death in 1892. His writing is characteristic of the Victorian era – formal, refined, rigorously metrical – and he was a favourite poet of Queen Victoria herself, who found his poems soothing after the death of her beloved husband Albert.

'Summer is coming, summer is coming.
  I know it, I know it, I know it.
Light again, leaf again, life again, love again,'
  Yes, my wild little Poet.

Sing the new year in under the blue.
  Last year you sang it as gladly.
'New, new, new, new'! Is it then *so* new
  That you should carol so madly?

'Love again, song again, nest again, young again,'
  Never a prophet so crazy!
And hardly a daisy as yet, little friend,
  See, there is hardly a daisy.

'Here again, here, here, here, happy year'!
  O warble unchidden, unbidden!
Summer is coming, is coming, my dear,
  And all the winters are hidden.

☾ 7 June · Swing Low, Sweet Chariot · Wallace Willis

Though in Britain 'Swing Low, Sweet Chariot' is best known as the England Rugby Team anthem, the song, or 'spiritual', was originally sung in the nineteenth century, by Black slaves, longing for freedom in the American South. Spirituals are a type of religious folksong, and this one is inspired by the Old Testament tale of Elijah, who was taken to heaven in a chariot. With its rocking rhythm and its promise of rest, this is also a perfect poem for the evening.

Swing low, sweet chariot
Coming for to carry me home,
Swing low, sweet chariot,
Coming for to carry me home.

I looked over Jordan, and what did I see
Coming for to carry me home?
A band of angels coming after me,
Coming for to carry me home.

Sometimes I'm up, and sometimes I'm down,
(Coming for to carry me home)
But still my soul feels heavenly bound.
(Coming for to carry me home)

The brightest day that I can say,
(Coming for to carry me home)
When Jesus washed my sins away.
(Coming for to carry me home)

If you get there before I do,
(Coming for to carry me home)
Tell all my friends I'm coming there too.
(Coming for to carry me home)

8 June · A London Plane-Tree · Amy Levy

The nineteenth-century poet Amy Levy was a radical.
A 'new woman', she lived a progressive life ahead of
her times. In this poem, both the poet and the tree are
cooped up in the city; the 'she' in the final stanza could
refer to either.

Green is the plane-tree in the square,
   The other trees are brown;
They droop and pine for country air;
   The plane-tree loves the town.

Here, from my garret-pane, I mark
   The plane-tree bud and blow,
Shed her recuperative bark,
   And spread her shade below.

Among her branches, in and out,
   The city breezes play;
The dun fog wraps her round about;
   Above, the smoke curls grey.

Others the country take for choice,
   And hold the town in scorn;
But she has listened to the voice
   On city breezes borne.

23

The title of this poem suggests both a lullaby that you sing to yourself, and a lullaby that is automatically generated by a machine rather than composed by a human – and this definition might explain the strange and unrelated pieces of advice that the poem gives.

> Think of a sheep
> knitting a sweater;
> think of your life
> getting better and better.
>
> Think of your cat
> asleep in a tree;
> think of that spot
> where you once skinned your knee.
>
> Think of a bird
> that stands in your palm.
> Try to remember
> the Twenty-first Psalm.
>
> Think of a big pink horse
> galloping south;
> think of a fly, and
> close your mouth.
>
> If you feel thirsty, then
> drink from your cup.
> The birds will keep singing
> until they wake up.

9 June · I Lost a World – the Other Day! · Emily Dickinson

It is not clear what, precisely, Emily Dickinson has lost in this poem – it could be anything from a book to a lover. What it makes clear, though, is that what is precious to one person might not be valuable to another.

I lost a World – the other day!
Has Anybody found?
You'll know it by the Row of Stars
Around its forehead bound.

A Rich man – might not notice it –
Yet – to my frugal Eye,
Of more Esteem than Ducats –
Oh find it – Sir – for me!

You may already know the lullaby 'Hush, Little Baby'. If you do, you will probably find it very hard to read it without humming along.

> Hush, little baby, don't say a word,
> Mama's gonna buy you a mockingbird.
> If that mockingbird don't sing,
> Mama's gonna buy you a diamond ring.
> If that diamond ring gets broke,
> Mama's gonna buy you a billy goat.
> If that billy goat won't pull,
> Mama's gonna buy you a cart and bull.
> If that cart and bull turn over,
> Mama's gonna buy you a dog named Rover.
> If that dog named Rover won't bark.
> Mama's gonna buy you a horse and cart.
> If that horse and cart fall down,
> You'll still be the sweetest little baby in town.
> So hush little baby don't you cry,
> 'Cause Daddy loves you and so do I.

Stevenson's poem takes a child's perspective on his or her own shadow – a shadow that seems to have a life of its own. It is strange to think that this is by the author of *Dr Jekyll and Mr Hyde*, a book in which the evil Hyde is like the shadowy side of the virtuous Jekyll.

I have a little shadow that goes in and out with me,
And what can be the use of him is more than I can see.
He is very, very like me from the heels up to the head;
And I see him jump before me, when I jump into my bed.

The funniest thing about him is the way he likes to grow –
Not at all like proper children, which is always very slow;
For he sometimes shoots up taller like an india-rubber
    ball,
And he sometimes gets so little that there's none of him
    at all.

He hasn't got a notion of how children ought to play,
And can only make a fool of me in every sort of way.
He stays so close beside me, he's a coward you can see;
I'd think shame to stick to nursie as that shadow sticks
    to me!

One morning, very early, before the sun was up,
I rose and found the shining dew on every buttercup;
But my lazy little shadow, like an arrant sleepy-head,
Had stayed at home behind me and was fast asleep in bed.

10 June · Sweet and Low (*from* The Princess) · Alfred, Lord Tennyson

This poem also works as a lullaby. If you read carefully it is clear that the poem is only partly about the child. The speaker of the poem is a lonely mother who is wishing for the return of the baby's father.

Sweet and low, sweet and low,
    Wind of the western sea,
Low, low, breathe and blow,
    Wind of the western sea!
Over the rolling waters go,
Come from the dying moon, and blow,
    Blow him again to me;
While my little one, while my pretty one, sleeps.

Sleep and rest, sleep and rest,
    Father will come to thee soon;
Rest, rest, on mother's breast,
    Father will come to thee soon;
Father will come to his babe in the nest,
Silver sails all out of the west
    Under the silver moon:
Sleep, my little one, sleep, my pretty one, sleep.

11 June · The Eagle · Alfred, Lord Tennyson

This is one of Tennyson's shortest poems and is, quite simply, a portrait of an eagle. We don't actually see the prey, but we can anticipate the inevitable swoop.

> He clasps the crag with crooked hands;
> Close to the sun in lonely lands,
> Ring'd with the azure world, he stands.
>
> The wrinkled sea beneath him crawls;
> He watches from his mountain walls,
> And like a thunderbolt he falls.

11 June · The End · A. A. Milne

This is one of Milne's best-known poems, and it is about his son, Christopher Robin. Its message is simple: that age is all a matter of perspective.

When I was One,
I had just begun.

When I was Two,
I was nearly new.

When I was Three,
I was hardly me.

When I was Four,
I was not much more.

When I was Five,
I was just alive.

But now I am Six, I'm as clever as clever
So I think I'll be six now for ever and ever.

Whereas A. A. Milne's poem, yesterday, took a
very straightforward approach to age, Billy Collins
complicates the emotions of growing older. Like Milne's
poem, it counts and catalogues age, but for Collins
everything looks different to the adult's eye.

The whole idea of it makes me feel
like I'm coming down with something,
something worse than any stomach ache
or the headaches I get from reading in bad light –
a kind of measles of the spirit,
a mumps of the psyche,
a disfiguring chicken pox of the soul.

You tell me it is too early to be looking back,
but that is because you have forgotten
the perfect simplicity of being one
and the beautiful complexity introduced by two.
But I can lie on my bed and remember every digit.
At four I was an Arabian wizard.
I could make myself invisible
by drinking a glass of milk a certain way.
At seven I was a soldier, at nine a prince.

But now I am mostly at the window
watching the late afternoon light.
Back then it never fell so solemnly
against the side of my tree house,
and my bicycle never leaned against the garage
as it does today,
all the dark blue speed drained out of it.

This is the beginning of sadness, I say to myself,
as I walk through the universe in my sneakers.
It is time to say good-bye to my imaginary friends,
time to turn the first big number.

It seems only yesterday I used to believe
there was nothing under my skin but light.
If you cut me I could shine.
But now when I fall upon the sidewalks of life,
I skin my knees. I bleed.

Sloths are mammals that live in trees in the jungles of Central and South America. They move very slowly, and only when it is absolutely necessary!

In moving slow he has no Peer.
You ask him something in his Ear,
He thinks about it for a Year;

And, then, before he says a Word
There, upside down (unlike a Bird),
He will assume that you have Heard

A most Ex-as-per-at-ing Lug.
But should you call his manner Smug,
He'll sigh and give his Branch a Hug;

Then off again to Sleep he goes,
Still swaying gently by his Toes,
And you just know he knows he knows.

13 June · The Pleasures of Friendship · Stevie Smith

Poems can be thousands of lines long, involving epic battles or describing fantastic worlds, like Milton's *Paradise Lost* or Homer's *Odyssey*. But some poems, like this one, are just a handful of words about one particularly special moment.

The pleasures of friendship are exquisite,
How pleasant to go to a friend on a visit!
I go to my friend, we walk on the grass,
And the hours and moments like minutes pass.

13 June · The Way Through the Woods · Rudyard Kipling

In this poem, Rudyard Kipling describes the scene of a tussle between human land-use and the wild, unordered forces of nature.

They shut the road through the woods
    Seventy years ago.
Weather and rain have undone it again,
    And now you would never know
There was once a road through the woods
    Before they planted the trees.
It is underneath the coppice and heath,
    And the thin anemones.
Only the keeper sees
    That, where the ring-dove broods,
And the badgers roll at ease,
    There was once a road through the woods.

Yet, if you enter the woods
    Of a summer evening late,
When the night-air cools on the trout-ringed pools
    Where the otter whistles his mate,
(They fear not men in the woods,
    Because they see so few)
You will hear the beat of a horse's feet
    And the swish of a skirt in the dew,
    Steadily cantering through
The misty solitudes,
    As though they perfectly knew
The old lost road through the woods . . .
But there is no road through the woods.

14 June · The Battle of Naseby · Thomas Babington Macaulay

The Battle of Naseby, on 14 June 1645, was a turning point in the English Civil War. The war was between Charles I and his Royalist supporters, and Oliver Cromwell's Parliamentarian forces. The Royalists lost most of their army and much of their supplies – their catastrophic defeat at Naseby led to the eventual execution of Charles I, and the rise of Cromwell as Lord Protector of England.

Oh! wherefore come ye forth in triumph from the north,
With your hands, and your feet, and your raiment all red?
And wherefore doth your rout send forth a joyous shout?
And whence be the grapes of the wine-press that ye tread?

Oh! evil was the root, and bitter was the fruit,
And crimson was the juice of the vintage that we trod;
For we trampled on the throng of the haughty and the
    strong,
Who sate in the high places and slew the saints of God.

It was about the noon of a glorious day of June,
That we saw their banners dance and their cuirasses
    shine,
And the man of blood was there, with his long essenced
    hair,
And Astley, and Sir Marmaduke, and Rupert of the Rhine.

36

Like a servant of the Lord, with his bible and his word,
The general rode along us to form us for the   fight;
When a murmuring sound broke out, and swell'd into a
    shout
Among the godless horsemen upon the tyrant's right.

And hark! like the roar of the billows on the shore,
The cry of battle rises along their charging line:
For God! for the cause! for the Church! for the laws!
For Charles, king of England, and Rupert of the Rhine!

The furious German comes, with his clarions and his drums,
His bravoes of Alsatia and pages of White-hall;
They are bursting on our flanks! Grasp your pikes! Close
    your ranks!
For Rupert never comes, but to conquer, or to fall.

They are here – they rush on – we are broken – we are
    gone –
Our left is borne before them like stubble on the blast.
O Lord, put forth Thy might! O Lord, defend the right!
Stand back to back, in God's name! and fight it to the last!

Stout Skippon hath a wound – the centre hath given
    ground.
Hark! hark! what means the trampling of horsemen on
    our rear?
Whose banner do I see, boys? 'T is he! thank God! 't is
    he, boys!
Bear up another minute! Brave Oliver is here!

Their heads all stooping low, their points all in a row:
Like a whirlwind on the trees, like a deluge on the dikes,
Our cuirassiers have burst on the ranks of the Accurst,
And at a shock have scatter'd the forest of his pikes

Fast, fast, the gallants ride, in some safe nook to hide
Their coward heads, predestin'd to rot on Temple Bar;
And he—he turns! he flies! shame on those cruel eyes
That bore to look on torture, and dare not look on war!

Ho, comrades! scour the plain; and ere ye strip the slain,
First give another stab to make your search secure;
Then shake from sleeves and pockets their broad-pieces
    and lockets,
The tokens of the wanton, the plunder of the poor.

Fools! your doublets shone with gold, and your hearts
    were gay and bold,
When you kiss'd your lily hands to your lemans to-day;
And to-morrow shall the fox from her chambers in the
    rocks
Lead forth her tawny cubs to howl about the prey.

Where be your tongues, that late mock'd at heaven and
    hell and fate?
And the fingers that once were so busy with your blades?
Your perfum'd satin clothes, your catches and your oaths?
Your stage-plays and your sonnets, your diamonds and
    your spades?

Down, down, for ever down with the mitre and the crown,
With the Belial of the court, and the Mammon of the Pope!
There is woe in Oxford halls, there is wail in Durham's
    stalls;
The Jesuit smites his bosom, the bishop rends his cope.

And she of the seven hills shall mourn her children's ills,
And tremble when she thinks on the edge of England's
    sword;
And the kings of earth in fear shall shudder when they
    hear
What the hand of God hath wrought for the Houses and
    the Word!

☾ 14 June · The Star-Spangled Banner · Francis Scott Key

In America, 14 June is Flag Day, the annual celebration of the date on which the Stars and Stripes were first adopted as the national emblem in 1777. This poem commemorates an early use of the American flag – also known as Old Glory and The Star-Spangled Banner – on the battlefield. Key wrote the poem after witnessing the Battle of Fort McHenry in 1814. Though he was being held captive on a British ship, Key watched through the night and was heartened to see the American flag still flying over the fort in the morning. The poem was set to music in the nineteenth century, but it did not become the official American national anthem until 1931.

O say, can you see, by the dawn's early light,
What so proudly we hailed at the twilight's last gleaming?
Whose broad stripes and bright stars through the
     perilous fight,
O'er the ramparts we watched were so gallantly streaming;
And the rocket's red glare, the bombs bursting in air,
Gave proof through the night that our flag was still there;
O say, does that star-spangled banner yet wave
O'er the land of the free, and the home of the brave?

On the shore dimly seen through the mists of the deep,
Where the foe's haughty host in dread silence reposes,
What is that which the breeze, o'er the towering steep,
As it fitfully blows, now conceals, now discloses?
Now it catches the gleam of the morning's first beam,
In full glory reflected now shines on the stream;
'Tis the star-spangled banner; O long may it wave
O'er the land of the free, and the home of the brave!

And where is that band who so vauntingly swore
That the havoc of war and the battle's confusion
A home and a country should leave us no more?
Their blood has washed out their foul footsteps' pollution.
No refuge could save the hireling and slave,
From the terror of flight and the gloom of the grave;
And the star-spangled banner in triumph doth wave
O'er the land of the free, and the home of the brave!

O! thus be it ever, when freemen shall stand
Between their loved homes and the war's desolation!
Blest with victory and peace, may the heav'n-rescued
    land
Praise the power that hath made and preserved us a
    nation.
Then conquer we must, for our cause it is just.
And this be our motto – 'In God is our trust';
And the star-spangled banner in triumph shall wave
O'er the land of the free, and the home of the brave.

15 June • Prayer Before Birth • Louis MacNeice

Poetry has the potential to offer us otherwise impossible perspectives, taking us inside the thoughts of those of other people and things. In this poem, it is an unborn baby who acts as narrator.

I am not yet born; O hear me.
Let not the bloodsucking bat or the rat or the stoat or the
    club-footed ghoul come near me.

I am not yet born, console me.
I fear that the human race may with tall walls wall me,
    with strong drugs dope me, with wise lies lure me,
    on black racks rack me, in blood-baths roll me.

I am not yet born; provide me
With water to dandle me, grass to grow for me, trees to
    talk to me, sky to sing to me, birds and a white light
    in the back of my mind to guide me.

I am not yet born; forgive me
For the sins that in me the world shall commit, my words
    when they speak me, my thoughts when they think me,
        my treason engendered by traitors beyond me,
            my life when they murder by means of my
                hands, my death when they live me.

I am not yet born; rehearse me
In the parts I must play and the cues I must take when
old men lecture me, bureaucrats hector me, mountains
frown at me, lovers laugh at me, the white
waves call me to folly and the desert calls
me to doom and the beggar refuses
my gift and my children curse me.
I am not yet born; O hear me,
Let not the man who is beast or who thinks he is God
come near me.

I am not yet born; O fill me
With strength against those who would freeze my
humanity, would dragoon me into a lethal automaton,
would make me a cog in a machine, a thing with
one face, a thing, and against all those
who would dissipate my entirety, would
blow me like thistledown hither and
thither or hither and thither
like water held in the
hands would spill me.

Let them not make me a stone and let them not spill me.
Otherwise kill me.

Rudyard Kipling

Runnymede is a water-meadow on the banks of the
River Thames, west of London, where – on 15 June
1215 – King John signed the document that came to be
known as Magna Carta, 'the great charter'. The charter
set limits on the power of the king.

At Runnymede, at Runnymede,
　　What say the reeds at Runnymede?
The lissom reeds that give and take,
That bend so far, but never break.
They keep the sleepy Thames awake
　　With tales of John at Runnymede.

At Runnymede, at Runnymede,
　　Oh, hear the reeds at Runnymede: –
'You mustn't sell, delay, deny,
A freeman's right or liberty.
It makes the stubborn Englishry,
　　We saw 'em roused at Runnymede!

'When through our ranks the Barons came,
With little thought of praise or blame,
But resolute to play the game,
　　They lumbered up to Runnymede;
And there they launched in solid line
The first attack on Right Divine –
The curt, uncompromising 'Sign!'
　　That settled John at Runnymede.

'At Runnymede, at Runnymede,
Your rights were won at Runnymede!
No freeman shall be fined or bound,
    Or dispossessed of freehold ground,
Except by lawful judgment found
And passed upon him by his peers.
Forget not, after all these years,
    The Charter Signed at Runnymede.'

And still when mob or monarch lays
Too rude a hand on English ways,
The whisper wakes, the shudder plays,
    Across the reeds at Runnymede.
And Thames, that knows the moods of kings,
And crowds and priests and suchlike things,
Rolls deep and dreadful as he brings
    Their warning down from Runnymede!

☀ **16 June** • Ecce Puer • James Joyce

The events of James Joyce's novel *Ulysses* all take place on one day, 16 June. For this reason, Dubliners and fans of literature commemorate the date, known as 'Bloomsday' (after its hero, Leopold Bloom), by reading aloud and publicly performing parts of the work. The title of this poem – 'Behold the boy' in Latin – is a play on the phrase 'Ecce Homo', Latin for 'Behold the man': the words spoken by Pontius Pilate as he presents Jesus to a crowd before his death on the cross. The poem marked both the birth of Joyce's grandson and the death of his own father. Joyce failed to return to Ireland when his father was dying, and in the final lines of 'Ecce Puer' he addresses his father and asks him to forgive him.

> Of the dark past
> A child is born.
> With joy and grief
> My heart is torn.
>
> Calm in his cradle
> The living lies.
> May love and mercy
> Unclose his eyes!
>
> Young life is breathed
> On the glass;
> The world that was not
> Comes to pass.

A child is sleeping:
An old man gone.
O, father forsaken,
Forgive your son!

W. B. Yeats claimed that the inspiration for 'The Lake Isle of Innisfree' came when he was walking down Fleet Street, London, in 1888 and was struck suddenly by a memory of his childhood. As a city boy he loved and longed for his summers in the countryside, especially the little island of Innisfree, on Lough Gill, an Irish lake in County Sligo.

I will arise and go now, and go to Innisfree,
And a small cabin build there, of clay and wattles made:
Nine bean-rows will I have there, a hive for the honey-bee,
And live alone in the bee-loud glade.

And I shall have some peace there, for peace comes
    dropping slow,
Dropping from the veils of the morning to where the
    cricket sings;
There midnight's all a glimmer, and noon a purple glow,
And evening full of the linnet's wings.

I will arise and go now, for always night and day
I hear lake water lapping with low sounds by the shore;
While I stand on the roadway, or on the pavements grey,
I hear it in the deep heart's core.

17 June · The Way Things Are ·
Roger McGough

The third Sunday in June is Father's Day in the UK and
the USA. It is a relatively new holiday, having only been
invented after the Second World War – but don't use
that as an excuse for forgetting it!

No, the candle is not crying, it cannot feel pain.
Even telescopes, like the rest of us, grow bored.
Bubblegum will not make the hair soft and shiny.
The duller the imagination, the faster the car,
I am your father and this is the way things are.

When the sky is looking the other way,
do not enter the forest. No, the wind
is not caused by the rushing of clouds.
An excuse is as good a reason as any.
A lighthouse, launched, will not go far,
I am your father and this is the way things are.

No, old people do not walk slowly
because they have plenty of time.
Gardening books when buried will not flower.
Though lightly worn, a crown may leave a scar,
I am your father and this is the way things are.

49

No, the red woolly hat has not been
put on the railing to keep it warm.
When one glove is missing, both are lost.
Today's craft fair is tomorrow's car boot sale.
The guitarist gently weeps, not the guitar,
I am your father and this is the way things are.

Pebbles work best without batteries.
The deckchair will fail as a unit of currency.
Even though your shadow is shortening
It does not mean you are growing smaller.
Moonbeams, sadly, will not survive in a jar,
I am your father and this is the way things are.

For centuries the bullet remained quietly confident
that the gun would be invented.
A drowning surrealist will not appreciate
the concrete life belt.
No guarantee my last goodbye is au revoir,
I am your father and this is the way things are.

Do not become a prison officer unless you know
what you're letting someone else in for.
The thrill of being a shower curtain will soon pall.
No trusting hand awaits the falling star,
I am your father, and I am sorry,
but this is the way things are.

17 June · *from* Childe Harold's Pilgrimage · George Gordon, Lord Byron

The English Romantic poet Lord Byron was notoriously eccentric, even keeping a bear in his rooms while he was a student at Trinity College, Cambridge. These stanzas are taken from his lengthy narrative poem, *Childe Harold's Pilgrimage*, which tells the story of a melancholic young man who, tired by a life of pleasure and excess, searches for distraction in foreign lands. The extract given here takes place on 17 June 1815, the eve of the Battle of Waterloo.

There was a sound of revelry by night,
And Belgium's Capital had gathered then
Her Beauty and her Chivalry, and bright
The lamps shone o'er fair women and brave men;
A thousand hearts beat happily; and when
Music arose with its voluptuous swell,
Soft eyes looked love to eyes which spake again,
And all went merry as a marriage bell;
But hush! hark! a deep sound strikes like a rising knell!

Did ye not hear it? – No; 'twas but the wind,
Or the car rattling o'er the stony street;
On with the dance! let joy be unconfined;
No sleep till morn, when Youth and Pleasure meet
To chase the glowing Hours with flying feet –
But hark! – that heavy sound breaks in once more,
As if the clouds its echo would repeat;
And nearer, clearer, deadlier than before!
Arm! Arm! it is – it is – the cannon's opening roar!

51

Within a windowed niche of that high hall
Sat Brunswick's fated chieftain; he did hear
That sound the first amidst the festival,
And caught its tone with Death's prophetic ear;
And when they smiled because he deemed it near,
His heart more truly knew that peal too well
Which stretched his father on a bloody bier,
And roused the vengeance blood alone could quell;
He rushed into the field, and, foremost fighting, fell.

18 June · *from* The Field of Waterloo · Sir Walter Scott

The Battle of Waterloo – the climactic moment of the Napoleonic wars, took place on 18 June 1815. Napoleon's army was defeated by British and Prussian armies, and the battle ended his long campaign to rule over all of Europe. These stanzas are from 'The Field of Waterloo' by the Scottish poet Sir Walter Scott. Scott created the poem out of descriptions of the battle given to him by those who fought there, with the aim of donating profits from the poem's sale to the soldiers. However, not everyone was impressed by his poem, as these scathing lines from a critic make clear: 'On Waterloo's ensanguin'd plain / Lie tens of thousands of the slain; / But none, by sabre or by shot, / Fell half so flat as Walter Scott.'

> Forgive, brave Dead, the imperfect lay!
> Who may your names, your numbers, say?
> What high-strung harp, what lofty line,
> To each the dear-earned praise assign,
> From high-born chiefs of martial fame
> To the poor soldier's lowlier name?
> Lightly ye rose that dawning day,
> From your cold couch of swamp and clay,
> To fill, before the sun was low,
> The bed that morning cannot know. –
> Oft may the tear the green sod steep,
> And sacred be the heroes' sleep,
>   Till time shall cease to run;

53

And ne'er beside their noble grave,
May Briton pass and fail to crave
A blessing on the fallen brave
    Who fought with Wellington!
Farewell, sad Field! whose blighted face
Wears desolation's withering trace;
Long shall my memory retain
Thy shatter'd huts and trampled grain,
With every mark of martial wrong,
That scathe thy towers, fair Hougomont!
Yet though thy garden's green arcade
The marksman's fatal post was made,
Though on thy shattered beeches fell
The blended rage of shot and shell,
Though from thy blacken'd portals torn,
Their fall thy blighted fruit-trees mourn,
Has not such havoc bought a name
Immortal in the rolls of fame?
Yes – Agincourt may be forgot,
And Cressy be an unknown spot,
    And Blenheim's name be new;
But still in story and in song,
For many an age remember'd long,
Shall live the towers of Hougomont,
    And fields of Waterloo.

18 June · The Sun Has Long Been Set · William Wordsworth

Following the defeat of the Emperor Napoleon at Waterloo, the Duke of Wellington – the commander of the British forces – reportedly said that the battle was 'the nearest-run thing you ever saw in your life'. This poem by William Wordsworth describes another night in June, questioning why any military parade would occur when there is such beauty in nature.

The sun has long been set,
  The stars are out by twos and threes,
The little birds are piping yet
  Among the bushes and trees;
There's a cuckoo, and one or two thrushes,
And a far-off wind that rushes,
And a sound of water that gushes,
And the cuckoo's sovereign cry
Fills all the hollow of the sky.
  Who would go 'parading'
In London, and 'masquerading',
On such a night of June
With that beautiful soft half-moon,
And all these innocent blisses?
On such a night as this is!

19 June • On Liberty and Slavery • George Moses Horton

On 19 June 1865 the inhuman institution of slavery was finally abolished in the USA, and millions of African-Americans were emancipated from the tyranny of subjugation. 19 June is known as 'Juneteenth' and is celebrated and recognized today in most American states. This powerful poem was written by George Moses Horton, who was born into servitude in 1798 on William Horton's plantation. He taught himself to read, and even managed to sell poems during his sixty-eight years of captivity, but he was not allowed to buy his freedom during this time. He is thought to have had at least seventeen years at the end of his life as a free man, as he died around 1883.

Alas! and am I born for this,
To wear this slavish chain?
Deprived of all created bliss,
Through hardship, toil and pain!

How long have I in bondage lain,
And languished to be free!
Alas! and must I still complain –
Deprived of liberty.

Oh, Heaven! and is there no relief
This side the silent grave –
To soothe the pain – to quell the grief
And anguish of a slave?

Come Liberty, thou cheerful sound,
Roll through my ravished ears!
Come, let my grief in joys be drowned,
And drive away my fears.

Say unto foul oppression, Cease:
Ye tyrants rage no more,
And let the joyful trump of peace,
Now bid the vassal soar.

Soar on the pinions of that dove
Which long has cooed for thee,
And breathed her notes from Afric's grove,
The sound of Liberty.

Oh, Liberty! thou golden prize,
So often sought by blood –
We crave thy sacred sun to rise,
The gift of nature's God!

Bid Slavery hide her haggard face,
And barbarism fly:
I scorn to see the sad disgrace
In which enslaved I lie.

Dear Liberty! upon thy breast,
I languish to respire;
And like the Swan unto her nest,
I'd like to thy smiles retire.

Oh, blest asylum – heavenly balm!
Unto thy boughs I flee –
And in thy shades the storm shall calm,
With songs of Liberty!

At the start of this poem Derek Walcott describes the type of lazy midsummer day that feels as if it will go on forever. What is surprising is the contrast between the first seven lines and the four that follow. Despite the sleepiness of the summer's day, the poet says time is racing by.

Broad sun-stoned beaches.

White heat.
A green river.

A bridge,
scorched yellow palms

from the summer-sleeping house
drowsing through August.

Days I have held,
days I have lost,

days that outgrow, like daughters,
my harbouring arms.

Paul Cookson is a British performance poet who writes mainly for children. Here he offers a child's perspective on the adult world, by focusing on one point of fascination: the father's hands.

Father's hands
large like frying pans
broad as shovel blades
strong as weathered spades.

Father's hands
finger ends ingrained with dirt
permanently stained from work
ignoring pain and scorning hurt.

I once saw him walk boldly up to a swan
that had landed in next door's drive and wouldn't move.
The police were there because swans are a protected
   species
but didn't do anything, but my dad walked up to it,
picked it up and carried it away. No problem.
Those massive wings that can break a man's bones
were held tight, tight by my father's hands
and I was proud of him that day, really proud.

Father's hands
tough as leather on old boots
firmly grasping nettle shoots
pulling thistles by their roots.

Father's hands
gripping like an iron vice
never numb in snow and ice
nails and screws are pulled and prised.

He once found a kestrel with a broken wing
and kept it in our garage until it was better.
He'd feed it by hand with scraps of meat or dead mice
and you could see where its beak and talons
had taken bits of skin from his finger ends.
It never seemed to hurt him at all, he just smiled
as he let it claw and peck.

Father's hands
lifting bales of hay and straw
calloused, hardened, rough and raw
building, planting, painting . . . more.

Father's hands
hard when tanning my backside
all we needed they supplied
and still my hands will fit inside

Father's hands
large like frying pans
broad as shovel blades
strong as weathered spades.

And still my hands will fit inside
my father's hands.

20 June is World Refugee Day. Brian Bilston's poem seems to offer an unsympathetic view of refugees, telling the reader not to help them – but try reading the poem again, this time from the bottom, and see if another view of the world might emerge.

They have no need of our help
So do not tell me
These haggard faces could belong to you or I
Should life have dealt a different hand
We need to see them for who they really are
Chancers and scroungers
Layabouts and loungers
With bombs up their sleeves
Cut-throats and thieves
They are not
Welcome here
We should make them
Go back to where they came from
They cannot
Share our food
Share our homes
Share our countries
Instead let us
Build a wall to keep them out
It is not okay to say
These are people just like us
A place should only belong to those who are born there
Do not be so stupid to think that
The world can be looked at another way

(Now read from bottom to top)

21 June · *from* A Midsummer Night's Dream · William Shakespeare

In the Northern Hemisphere, 21 June is the Summer Solstice. Also known as Midsummer Day, it is the longest day of the year as the Earth's tilt is most inclined towards the sun. Shakespeare's *A Midsummer Night's Dream* preserves the magic and mystery with which the day has been enshrouded for thousands of years. Here Duke Theseus delivers a meditation on what it means to dream – or to imagine.

> More strange than true! I never may believe
> These antique fables, nor these fairy toys.
> Lovers and madmen have such seething brains,
> Such shaping fantasies, that apprehend
> More than cool reason ever comprehends.
> The lunatic, the lover and the poet
> Are of imagination all compact.
> One sees more devils than vast hell can hold:
> That is the madman. The lover, all as frantic,
> Sees Helen's beauty in a brow of Egypt.
> The poet's eye, in fine frenzy rolling,
> Doth glance from heaven to earth, from earth to heaven,
> And as imagination bodies forth
> The forms of things unknown, the poet's pen
> Turns them to shapes, and gives to airy nothing
> A local habitation and a name.
> Such tricks hath strong imagination,
> That if it would but apprehend some joy,
> It comprehends some bringer of that joy;
> Or in the night, imagining some fear,
> How easy is a bush suppos'd a bear!

21 June • *from* A Midsummer Night's Dream • William Shakespeare

A Midsummer Night's Dream takes place in and around ancient Athens where the Solstice was customarily celebrated as an important pagan festival. Bonfires were traditionally lit to protect against evil spirits which pagans believed were free to wander the earth on this auspicious date. Shakespeare's comedy, with its cast of fairies and plot suffused with magic, taps into the tradition of Midsummer as a date on which remarkable things can happen.

I know a bank where the wild thyme blows,
Where oxlips and the nodding violet grows,
Quite over-canopied with luscious woodbine,
With sweet musk-roses and with eglantine:
There sleeps Titania sometime of the night,
Lull'd in these flowers with dances and delight;
And there the snake throws her enamell'd skin,
Weed wide enough to wrap a fairy in:
And with the juice of this I'll streak her eyes,
And make her full of hateful fantasies.
Take thou some of it, and seek through this grove:
A sweet Athenian lady is in love
With a disdainful youth: anoint his eyes;
But do it when the next thing he espies
May be the lady: thou shalt know the man
By the Athenian garments he hath on.
Effect it with some care, that he may prove
More fond on her than she upon her love:
And look thou meet me ere the first cock crow.

63

22 June · Recessional · Rudyard Kipling

On 22 June 1897, Queen Victoria celebrated her
Diamond Jubilee. It marked her sixtieth year on the
throne, and meant that she surpassed George III as
the longest ever reigning monarch of Great Britain – a
record overtaken by Queen Elizabeth II in 2015. This
poem by Kipling was written for Victoria's Diamond
Jubilee. A 'recessional' is a type of hymn, and the poem
is accordingly more solemn than it is celebratory.
The poem, which expresses some pride in the British
Empire, suggests that even the longest reigns must end,
and it repeats the now-famous phrase 'Lest we forget'.

God of our fathers, known of old,
    Lord of our far-flung battle-line,
Beneath whose awful Hand we hold
    Dominion over palm and pine –
Lord God of Hosts, be with us yet,
Lest we forget – lest we forget!

The tumult and the shouting dies;
    The Captains and the Kings depart:
Still stands Thine ancient sacrifice,
    An humble and a contrite heart.
Lord God of Hosts, be with us yet,
Lest we forget – lest we forget!

Far-called, our navies melt away;
  On dune and headland sinks the fire:
Lo, all our pomp of yesterday
  Is one with Nineveh and Tyre!
Judge of the Nations, spare us yet,
Lest we forget – lest we forget!

If, drunk with sight of power, we loose
  Wild tongues that have not Thee in awe,
Such boastings as the Gentiles use,
  Or lesser breeds without the Law –
Lord God of Hosts, be with us yet,
Lest we forget – lest we forget!

For heathen heart that puts her trust
  In reeking tube and iron shard,
All valiant dust that builds on dust,
  And guarding, calls not Thee to guard,
For frantic boast and foolish word –
Thy mercy on Thy People, Lord!

Amen.

☾ 22 June • *from* As You Like It • William Shakespeare

This famous speech from *As You Like It* is given by the character Jaques. As a comedy, *As You Like It* is for the most part a light-hearted play. Jaques, however, is notably melancholic, and his speeches are reflective and philosophical in tone.

> All the world's a stage,
> And all the men and women merely players;
> They have their exits and their entrances;
> And one man in his time plays many parts,
> His acts being seven ages. At first the infant,
> Mewling and puking in the nurse's arms;
> And then the whining school-boy, with his satchel
> And shining morning face, creeping like snail
> Unwillingly to school. And then the lover,
> Sighing like furnace, with a woeful ballad
> Made to his mistress' eyebrow. Then a soldier,
> Full of strange oaths, and bearded like the pard,
> Jealous in honour, sudden and quick in quarrel,
> Seeking the bubble reputation
> Even in the cannon's mouth. And then the justice,
> In fair round belly with good capon lin'd,
> With eyes severe and beard of formal cut,
> Full of wise saws and modern instances;
> And so he plays his part. The sixth age shifts
> Into the lean and slipper'd pantaloon,
> With spectacles on nose and pouch on side;
> His youthful hose, well sav'd, a world too wide

For his shrunk shank; and his big manly voice,
Turning again toward childish treble, pipes
And whistles in his sound. Last scene of all,
That ends this strange eventful history,
Is second childishness and mere oblivion;
Sans teeth, sans eyes, sans taste, sans everything.

23 June · The Land of the Bumbley Boo · Spike Milligan

23 June 2016, was the day on which the British public voted to exit the European Union. Spike Milligan's poem may seem like complete nonsense, but it might not be. In a land where the people are red, white and blue – the colours of the Union Jack – Bumbley Boo might be closer to home than we at first think.

In the Land of the Bumbley Boo
The People are red, white and blue,
They never blow noses,
Or ever wear closes,
What a sensible thing to do!

In the Land of the Bumbley Boo
You can buy Lemon pie at the Zoo,
They give away Foxes
In little Pink Boxes
And Bottles of Dandylion Stew.

In the Land of the Bumbley Boo
You never see a Gnu,
But thousands of cats
Wearing trousers and hats
Made of Pumpkins and Pelican Glue!

Oh, the Bumbley Boo! the Bumbley Boo!
That's the place for me and you!
So hurry! Let's run!
The train leaves at one!
For the Land of the Bumbley Boo!
The wonderful Bumbley Boo-Boo-Boo!
The Wonderful Bumbley BOO!!!

Nearly all the great poets, from the Roman Horace to Shakespeare, Andrew Marvell to A. E. Housman, Robert Herrick to Percy Bysshe Shelley, have written on the need to seize the day in the face of life's fleeting nature. The American Pulitzer Prize-winning writer Mary Oliver joins that illustrious list with her own wonderful *carpe diem* poem. But rather than exhorting the reader to throw themselves into all manner of activities, Oliver draws attention to the simple pleasures and everyday miracles that we can too often overlook – in this instance a grasshopper going about its usual business.

Who made the world?
Who made the swan, and the black bear?
Who made the grasshopper?
This grasshopper, I mean –
the one who has flung herself out of the grass,
the one who is eating sugar out of my hand,
who is moving her jaws back and forth instead of up
    and down –
who is gazing around with her enormous and
    complicated eyes.
Now she lifts her pale forearms and thoroughly
    washes her face.
Now she snaps her wings open, and floats away.
I don't know exactly what a prayer is.
I do know how to pay attention, how to fall down
into the grass, how to kneel down in the grass,
how to be idle and blessed, how to stroll through the
    fields,

which is what I have been doing all day.
Tell me, what else should I have done?
Doesn't everything die at last, and too soon?
Tell me, what is it you plan to do
with your one wild and precious life?

24 June · The Fiddler of Dooney · W. B. Yeats

Yeats's fiddler has proven such a popular figure that there is a real 'Fiddler of Dooney Competition' held each year in Sligo, the town mentioned in the poem that sits alongside Dooney Rock hill. In the spirit of the poem, it is a celebration of the joy of traditional folk music and dancing.

When I play my fiddle in Dooney,
Folk dance like a wave of the sea;
My cousin is a priest in Kilvarnet,
My brother in Mocharabuiee.

I passed my brother and cousin:
They read in their books of prayer;
I read in my book of songs
I bought at the Sligo fair.

When we come to the end of time
To Peter sitting in state,
He will smile on three old spirits,
But call me first through the gate;

For the good are always the merry,
Save for an evil chance,
And the merry love the fiddle,
And the merry love to dance:

And when the folk there spy me,
They will all come up to me,
With 'Here is the fiddler of Dooney!'
And dance like a wave of the sea.

72

☾ 24 June · Adlestrop · Edward Thomas

On 24 June 1914, the poet Edward Thomas was
travelling from London to his friend and fellow poet
Robert Frost's house near Ledbury when the steam
train he was on made an unscheduled stop at a
Gloucestershire hamlet called Adlestrop. This brief visit
provided the inspiration for this poem. Thomas was
greatly inspired by nature, and in his notebook, writing
about the stop in Adlestrop, he scribbled: '. . . thro the
willows cd be heard a chain of blackbird songs at 12.45,
and one thrush and no man seen, only a hiss of engine
letting off steam.'

Yes. I remember Adlestrop –
The name – because one afternoon
Of heat the express-train drew up there
Unwontedly. It was late June.

The steam hissed. Someone cleared his throat.
No one left and no one came
On the bare platform. What I saw
Was Adlestrop – only the name –

And willows, willow-herb, and grass,
And meadowsweet, and haycocks dry;
No whit less still and lonely fair
Than the high cloudlets in the sky.

And for that minute a blackbird sang
Close by, and round him, mistier,
Farther and farther, all the birds
Of Oxfordshire and Gloucestershire.

25 June • My Mother Saw a Dancing Bear • Charles Causley

On this day in 1824, the Royal Society for the Protection of Animals, or RSPCA, was founded in a coffee shop. It was the first animal charity in the world. At first it wasn't 'royal' at all, until Queen Victoria granted it royal status in 1840. Causley's poem about a dancing bear (or 'bruin'), and how it dreams for its far-off home, offers no overt judgement about the scene but makes a quiet statement about animal cruelty.

My mother saw a dancing bear
By the schoolyard, a day in June.
The keeper stood with chain and bar
And whistle-pipe, and played a tune.

And bruin lifted up its head
And lifted up its dusty feet,
And all the children laughed to see
It caper in the summer heat.

They watched as for the Queen it died.
They watched it march. They watched it halt.
They heard the keeper as he cried,
'Now, roly-poly!' 'Somersault!'

And then, my mother said, there came
The keeper with a begging-cup,
The bear with burning coat of fur,
Shaming the laughter to a stop.

They paid a penny for the dance,
But what they saw was not the show;
Only, in bruin's aching eyes,
Far-distant forests, and the snow.

☾ 25 June · The Cat and the Moon · W. B. Yeats

This mysterious, deceptively simple poem plays with the similarity between a cat's eyes and the changing shapes of the moon.

The cat went here and there
And the moon spun round like a top,
And the nearest kin of the moon,
The creeping cat, looked up.
Black Minnaloushe stared at the moon,
For, wander and wail as he would,
The pure cold light in the sky
Troubled his animal blood.
Minnaloushe runs in the grass
Lifting his delicate feet.
Do you dance, Minnaloushe, do you dance?
When two close kindred meet,
What better than call a dance?
Maybe the moon may learn,
Tired of that courtly fashion,
A new dance turn.
Minnaloushe creeps through the grass
From moonlit place to place,
The sacred moon overhead
Has taken a new phase.
Does Minnaloushe know that his pupils
Will pass from change to change,
And that from round to crescent,
From crescent to round they range?
Minnaloushe creeps through the grass
Alone, important and wise,
And lifts to the changing moon
His changing eyes.

26 June · At the Railway Station, Upway · Thomas Hardy

Thomas Hardy was one of the most celebrated novelists of the nineteenth and twentieth centuries, but he saw himself primarily as a poet. In both his fiction and his verse, he sought to create realistic depictions of life in Victorian England, including the controversial topics of poverty and crime. Upway is a railway station in Dorset, where Hardy spent most of his life, and where many of his literary works were set.

'There is not much that I can do,
For I've no money that's quite my own!'
Spoke up the pitying child –
A little boy with a violin
At the station before the train came in, –
'But I can play my fiddle to you,
And a nice one 'tis, and good in tone!'

The man in the handcuffs smiled;
The constable looked, and he smiled, too,
As the fiddle began to twang;
And the man in the handcuffs suddenly sang
With grimful glee:
'This life so free
Is the thing for me!'
And the constable smiled, and said no word,
As if unconscious of what he heard;
And so they went on till the train came in –
The convict, and boy with the violin.

77

In just two stanzas and eight lines, the early twentieth-century poet Sara Teasdale evokes the euphonious delights of birdsong on a summer evening, and the ethereal quality of the sky as the day slowly gives way to night. In the last lines Teasdale gently implores us to make the most of such vibrant moments before darkness falls – perhaps a tacit metaphor for life itself.

Evening, and all the birds
In a chorus of shimmering sound
Are easing their hearts of joy
For miles around.

The air is blue and sweet,
The few first stars are white,--
Oh let me like the birds
Sing before night.

This poem tells a story that might be all too familiar
to you – and to your parents – if you've ever been on a
long car journey with your family.

Mum says:
'Right, you two,
this is a very long car journey.
I want you two to be good.
I'm driving and I can't drive properly
if you two are going mad in the back.
Do you understand?'

So we say,
'OK, Mum, OK. Don't worry,'
and off we go.

And we start The Moaning:
Can I have a drink?
I want some crisps.
Can I open my window?
He's got my book.
Get off me.
Ow, that's my ear!

And Mum tries to be exciting:
'Look out the window
there's a lamp-post.'

And we go on with The Moaning:
Can I have a sweet?
He's sitting on me.
Are we nearly there?
Don't scratch.
You never tell him off.
Now he's biting his nails.
I want a drink. I want a drink.
And Mum tries to be exciting again:
'Look out the window.
There's a tree.'

And we go on:
My hands are sticky.
He's playing with the doorhandle now.
I feel sick.
Your nose is all runny.
Don't pull my hair.

He's touching me, Mum.
That's really dangerous, you know.
Mum, he's spitting.

And Mum says:
'Right I'm stopping the car.
I AM STOPPING THE CAR.'

She stops the car.

'Now, if you two don't stop it
I'm going to put you out of the car
and leave you by the side of the road.'

He started it.
I didn't. He started it.

'I don't care who started it
I can't drive properly
if you two go mad in the back.
Do you understand?'

And we say:
OK, Mum, OK, don't worry.

Can I have a drink?

In this compassionate poem, the poet Laura Mucha
conjures up 'The Land of Blue': an imaginary place
which characterizes how it might feel if you, or someone
you know, feels sad or blue.

Across the valley, it waits for you,
a place they call The Land of Blue.

It's far and near, it's strange yet known –
and in this land, you'll feel alone,
you might feel tears roll down your cheek,
you might feel wobbly, weary, weak.

I know this won't sound fun to you –
it's not – this is The Land of Blue.
It's blue – not gold or tangerine,
it's dark – not light, not bright or clean.

It's blue – and when you leave, you'll see
the crackly branches of the tree,
the golden skies, the purring cat,
the piercing eyes, the feathered hat
and all the other things that come
when you escape from feeling glum.

Across the valley, it waits for you,
a place they call The Land of Blue
and going there will help you know
how others feel when they feel low.

28 June · A Bird Came Down the Walk · Emily Dickinson

This poem is an excellent example of Dickinson's brilliant use of poetic metre to create a songlike effect. There are six pairs of unstressed and stressed syllables to each line, and she divides these into groups, or stanzas, of four lines. Dickinson also coins the imaginative word 'plashless' at the end to describe a butterfly swimming in air rather than water.

A Bird came down the Walk –
He did not know I saw –
He bit an Angleworm in halves
And ate the fellow, raw,

And then he drank a Dew
From a convenient Grass –
And then hopped sidewise to the Wall
To let a Beetle pass –

He glanced with rapid eyes
That hurried all around –
They looked like frightened Beads, I thought –
He stirred his Velvet Head

Like one in danger, Cautious,
I offered him a Crumb
And he unrolled his feathers
And rowed him softer home –

Than Oars divide the Ocean,
Too silver for a seam –
Or Butterflies, off Banks of Noon
Leap, plashless as they swim.

☾ 28 June • June • John Updike

This poem is taken from the Pulitzer Prize-winning author John Updike's little-known book of children's poems, *A Child's Calendar*. In it Updike writes a poem for every month of the year.

> The sun is rich
> And gladly pays
> In golden hours,
> Silver days,
>
> And long green weeks
> That never end.
> School's out. The time
> Is ours to spend.
>
> There's Little League,
> Hopscotch, the creek,
> And, after supper,
> Hide-and-seek.
>
> The live-long light
> Is like a dream,
> and freckles come
> Like flies to cream.

Here is a poem by the former Poet Laureate on the subject of moving home. Collecting the memories of relocating, as a youngster, from Glasgow, Scotland to Stafford in England, Duffy comes to reflect that 'All childhood is an emigration' – we are always on the move as we grow up.

We came from our own country in a red room
which fell through the fields, our mother singing
our father's name to the turn of the wheels.
My brothers cried, one of them bawling, *Home,*
Home, as the miles rushed back to the city,
the street, the house, the vacant rooms
where we didn't live any more. I stared
at the eyes of a blind toy, holding its paw.

All childhood is an emigration. Some are slow,
leaving you standing, resigned, up an avenue
where no one you know stays. Others are sudden.
Your accent wrong. Corners, which seem familiar,
leading to unimagined, pebble-dashed estates, big boys
eating worms and shouting words you don't understand.
My parents' anxiety stirred like a loose tooth
in my head. *I want our own country*, I said.

But then you forget, or don't recall, or change,
and, seeing your brother swallow a slug, feel only
a skelf of shame. I remember my tongue
shedding its skin like a snake, my voice
in the classroom sounding just like the rest. Do I only
    think
I lost a river, culture, speech, sense of first space
and the right place? Now, *Where do you come from?*
strangers ask. *Originally?* And I hesitate.

☽ **29 June** · *from* Childe Harold's Pilgrimage · George Gordon, Lord Byron

Lord Byron was in many sense the first modern celebrity. He was controversial and outrageous, spending fortunes on his lavish lifestyle and attracting a large number of female admirers. Though he remained always a man of leisure, he was an extremely accomplished swimmer and boxer (not to mention poet), and he eventually died after falling ill in Greece, whilst while helping to mobilize the forces for Greek independence. The long, episodic poem *Childe Harold's Pilgrimage* was a bestseller in its day, and it tells fictionalized versions of many of Byron's own adventures.

There is a pleasure in the pathless woods,
There is a rapture on the lonely shore,
There is society where none intrudes,
By the deep Sea, and music in its roar:
I love not Man the less, but Nature more,
From these our interviews, in which I steal
From all I may be, or have been before,
To mingle with the Universe, and feel
What I can ne'er express, yet cannot all conceal.

Roll on, thou deep and dark blue Ocean – roll!
Ten thousand fleets sweep over thee in vain;
Man marks the earth with ruin – his control
Stops with the shore; – upon the watery plain
The wrecks are all thy deed, nor doth remain
A shadow of man's ravage, save his own,
When, for a moment, like a drop of rain,
He sinks into thy depths with bubbling groan,
Without a grave, unknell'd, uncoffin'd, and unknown.

His steps are not upon thy paths, – thy fields
Are not a spoil for him, – thou dost arise
And shake him from thee; the vile strength he wields
For earth's destruction thou dost all despise,
Spurning him from thy bosom to the skies,
And send'st him, shivering in thy playful spray
And howling, to his Gods, where haply lies
His petty hope in some near port or bay,
And dashest him again to earth: – there let him lay.

Here is another poem by a former Poet Laureate, and
like Carol Ann Duffy's 'Originally', this one by Tennyson
is also about home. 'Ulysses' is the Latin name for
Odysseus, the hero of one of the oldest poems in the
world, the *Odyssey* of Homer. Homer's work follows
Odysseus on his long and dangerous return home to
Ithaca after the Trojan War. In Tennyson's poem, the
heroic Ulysses finds he is not fit to be at home, and he
yearns to head out on another adventure. The final,
very beautiful, lines are particularly famous – they even
feature in the James Bond film, *Skyfall*!

It little profits that an idle king,
By this still hearth, among these barren crags,
Match'd with an aged wife, I mete and dole
Unequal laws unto a savage race,
That hoard, and sleep, and feed, and know not me.
I cannot rest from travel: I will drink
Life to the lees: All times I have enjoy'd
Greatly, have suffer'd greatly, both with those
That loved me, and alone, on shore, and when
Thro' scudding drifts the rainy Hyades
Vext the dim sea: I am become a name;
For always roaming with a hungry heart
Much have I seen and known; cities of men
And manners, climates, councils, governments,
Myself not least, but honour'd of them all;
And drunk delight of battle with my peers,
Far on the ringing plains of windy Troy.
I am a part of all that I have met;

Yet all experience is an arch wherethro'
Gleams that untravell'd world whose margin fades
For ever and for ever when I move.
How dull it is to pause, to make an end,
To rust unburnish'd, not to shine in use!
As tho' to breathe were life. Life piled on life
Were all too little, and of one to me
Little remains: but every hour is saved
From that eternal silence, something more,
A bringer of new things; and vile it were
For some three suns to store and hoard myself,
And this gray spirit yearning in desire
To follow knowledge like a sinking star,
Beyond the utmost bound of human thought.
   This is my son, mine own Telemachus,
To whom I leave the sceptre and the isle, –
Well-loved of me, discerning to fulfil
This labour, by slow prudence to make mild
A rugged people, and thro' soft degrees
Subdue them to the useful and the good.
Most blameless is he, centred in the sphere
Of common duties, decent not to fail
In offices of tenderness, and pay
Meet adoration to my household gods,
When I am gone. He works his work, I mine.
   There lies the port; the vessel puffs her sail:
There gloom the dark, broad seas. My mariners,
Souls that have toil'd, and wrought, and thought with
      me –
That ever with a frolic welcome took
The thunder and the sunshine, and opposed
Free hearts, free foreheads – you and I are old;
Old age hath yet his honour and his toil;
Death closes all: but something ere the end,

Some work of noble note, may yet be done,
Not unbecoming men that strove with Gods.
The lights begin to twinkle from the rocks:
The long day wanes: the slow moon climbs: the deep
Moans round with many voices. Come, my friends,
'Tis not too late to seek a newer world.
Push off, and sitting well in order smite
The sounding furrows; for my purpose holds
To sail beyond the sunset, and the baths
Of all the western stars, until I die.
It may be that the gulfs will wash us down:
It may be we shall touch the Happy Isles,
And see the great Achilles, whom we knew.
Tho' much is taken, much abides; and tho'
We are not now that strength which in old days
Moved earth and heaven, that which we are, we are;
One equal temper of heroic hearts,
Made weak by time and fate, but strong in will
To strive, to seek, to find, and not to yield.

On 30 June 1905, the theoretical physicist Albert Einstein published the 'Theory of Special Relativity', which included his most famous equation, $E = mc^2$, meaning that there is an equivalence between a body's mass and energy. Like Ulysses, Einstein's life was defined by the indefatigable spirit of a hero who has the drive to keep pushing himself, to keep seeking uncharted territories. His explorations were of a theoretical nature, but his work on light, matter, gravity, space, and time, have sharpened and shaped our understanding of the world.

I heard that they've got Einstein's brain
just sitting in a jar.
I don't know where they keep it,
but I hope it isn't far.

I need to go and borrow it
to help me with this test.
I've answered twenty questions
but on every one I guessed.
If someone asks you where I've gone,
then kindly please explain
I'll be right back; I've just gone out
to look for Einstein's brain.

July

☀ 1 July · Remembered More for His Beard Now · Philip Ardagh

On 1 July 1858, Charles Darwin presented his and Alfred Russel Wallace's Theory of Evolution to a London scientific society. The presentation led Darwin to write *On the Origin of Species*, cementing his place in the history of science and our understanding of ourselves. Not everyone in Victorian times found it easy to accept that man shared a common ancestor with apes – nor that we were not created by God.

Remembered more for his beard now,
Bushy and white.
A touch of Father Christmas
On a face as stern as sandpaper
Taking no prisoners.
Never young.

Misremembered as having stated
That Man is descended from apes,
Causing some to query
Why it is
That the mating pair of gorillas
At the Royal Zoological Gardens
Has yet to give birth to
A young accountant.

When reminded that his actual conclusion is that
We share a common ancestry with apes,
There is outrage in SW19,
Where the only thing 'common' about them,
Or so they claim,

95

Is to be found as a patch of greenery in Wimbledon
(Since overrun with Wombles).
Reviled by those of faith,
Or those who hide behind it,
Darwin is also needled by those scientists
Who question his assertion as to
The Survival of the Fittest.
But soon his theories evolve into
The accepted norm,
Trampling detractors underfoot,
Their weak protestations taking one final, gasping breath.

When, at the behest of Her Majesty's Royal Mail,
His home village of Down
Evolves into Downe with a tail
In the form of a letter 'e',
Darwin stands firm.
His residence, Down House,
Remains unchanged.

Not unlike a dinosaur, with eyes tight shut,
A clawed finger in either ear; and humming loudly,
He attempts to postpone the inevitable,
Simply by denying that he can see it coming.
Yet Down House, with no 'e', it remains
To this day.

To the victor the spoils.

Closer inspection of Darwin's portraits reveals kind eyes.
Humanity amongst the facial hair,
Like the white-haired God of Sunday school.
Both worshipped by different congregations.
Forever and ever.
Charles Darwin.

The invention of Edmund Clerihew Bentley, a 'clerihew' is a short comic poem which provides some form of comment on a famous figure's name and biography. This one rests on the pun that venison is both dear – that is, expensive – and deer. The 1st of July is the start of the deer-stalking season in Scotland.

> Alfred, Lord Tennyson
> Lived upon venison;
> Not cheap, I fear,
> Because venison's deer.

2 July · Wolfgang Amadeus Mozart · E. C. Bentley

This clerihew takes as its subject one of the most celebrated composers of Western Classical music, Wolfgang Amadeus Mozart. Although he died at the age of only 36, he was hugely prolific in his lifetime, composing 41 symphonies, 27 piano concertos and 22 operas. The unusual word 'otophagic' means 'painful to the ear', and the poem puns on the title of one of Mozart's most popular operas: *The Magic Flute*.

> Wolfgang Amadeus Mozart
> Whose very name connotes art
> Thought flutes untunable and otophagic
> Till he made one that was magic.

Amelia Earhart was an American pilot who, in 1932, became the first woman to fly solo across the Atlantic Ocean. On 2 July 1937 she disappeared during an attempt to fly around the globe, losing radio contact and vanishing somewhere over the Pacific. No trace was ever found of her or her plane.

> '... *fears are paper tigers.*'

A ribbon in her hair and mud on her dress
Amelia climbs too high
then, like any child in a tree,
blinks at the dizzying ground and sky.

Amelia spreads the map on her knees
to light the Atlantic with her torch.
She taps the fuel gauge, adjusts her course.
The stars seemed near enough to touch.

Amelia's red Vega roars around
a world of cloud and sun and time,
and whenever a child defeats
her fears, Amelia still climbs.

☀ 3 July · Solitude · Ella Wheeler Wilcox

This poem is considered by many to be Ella Wheeler Wilcox's finest, and its opening lines are often quoted, frequently parodied, and highly memorable.

> Laugh, and the world laughs with you;
> Weep, and you weep alone;
> For the sad old earth must borrow its mirth,
> But has trouble enough of its own.
> Sing, and the hills will answer;
> Sigh, it is lost on the air;
> The echoes bound to a joyful sound,
> But shrink from voicing care.
>
> Rejoice, and men will seek you;
> Grieve, and they turn and go;
> They want full measure of all your pleasure,
> But they do not need your woe.
> Be glad, and your friends are many;
> Be sad, and you lose them all, –
> There are none to decline your nectared wine,
> But alone you must drink life's gall.
>
> Feast, and your halls are crowded;
> Fast, and the world goes by.
> Succeed and give, and it helps you live,
> But no man can help you die.
> There is room in the halls of pleasure
> For a large and lordly train,
> But one by one we must all file on
> Through the narrow aisles of pain.

3 July • *from* An Essay on Criticism • Alexander Pope

The eighteenth-century English poet and master of wit Alexander Pope wrote much that is memorable: 'To err is human; to forgive, divine,' 'A little learning is a dang'rous thing,' and 'For fools rush in where angels fear to tread' are just some of his most quoted lines. He was best-known for his satirical heroic couplets. Here he launches an attack on bad, predictable writing.

And ten low Words oft creep in one dull Line,
While they ring round the same *unvary'd Chimes*,
With sure *Returns* of still *expected Rhymes*.
Where-e'er you find *the cooling Western Breeze*,
In the next Line, it *whispers thro' the Trees*;
If *Crystal Streams with pleasing Murmurs creep*,
The Reader's threaten'd (not in vain) with *Sleep*.

4 July • For You O Democracy • Walt Whitman

4 July is American Independence Day. On this day in 1776, during the Revolutionary War against Great Britain, the Declaration of Independence was signed and passed in Philadelphia, marking the birth of the United States of America. People now celebrate the day with firework displays, parades and family reunions. Whitman's poem is a celebration of togetherness and companionship, the glue that holds together American democracy.

Come, I will make the continent indissoluble,
I will make the most splendid race the sun ever shone
    upon,
I will make divine magnetic lands,
        With the love of comrades,
          With the life-long love of comrades.

I will plant companionship thick as trees along all the
    rivers of America, and along the shores of the great
    lakes, and all over the prairies,
I will make inseparable cities with their arms about
    each other's necks,
        By the love of comrades,
          By the manly love of comrades.

For you these from me, O Democracy, to serve you ma
    femme!
For you, for you I am trilling these songs.

🌙 4 July · I Hear America Singing · Walt Whitman

The United States is still a relatively young country but it already has a rich and established poetic tradition. Born forty-three years after the Declaration of Independence, Walt Whitman would certainly feature in any discussion of the nation's most influential literary figures, and he has been referred to as 'America's first democratic poet' and 'America's world poet'. This is one of many poems in which he expounded his thoughts on what it means to be American and in which he immortalizes his fellow citizens. Whitman himself called America the 'greatest poem' and so it's only fitting to read a piece by him on the country's most significant anniversary.

I hear America singing, the varied carols I hear,
Those of mechanics, each one singing his as it should be
     blithe and strong,
The carpenter singing his as he measures his plank or
     beam,
The mason singing his as he makes ready for work, or
     leaves off work,
The boatman singing what belongs to him in his boat,
     the deckhand singing on the steamboat deck,
The shoemaker singing as he sits on his bench, the
     hatter singing as he stands,
The wood-cutter's song, the ploughboy's on his way in
     the morning, or at noon intermission or at sundown,

The delicious singing of the mother, or of the young wife
    at work, or of the girl sewing or washing,
Each singing what belongs to him or her and to none else,
The day what belongs to the day—at night the party of
    young fellows, robust, friendly,
Singing with open mouths their strong melodious songs.

5 July · The Tables Turned · William Wordsworth

As the school year comes to a close, you might need to be reminded to stop studying (or you might not). In Wordsworth's poem, the narrator teaches his friend that it can be good to close your textbooks, and to learn from the book of nature instead. The poem is known for the much-quoted criticism of science, 'We murder to dissect', and the description of dull books as 'those barren leaves' was used as the title of a novel by Aldous Huxley, the author of *Brave New World*.

Up! up! my Friend, and quit your books;
Or surely you'll grow double:
Up! up! my Friend, and clear your looks;
Why all this toil and trouble?

The sun above the mountain's head,
A freshening lustre mellow
Through all the long green fields has spread,
His first sweet evening yellow.

Books! 'tis a dull and endless strife:
Come, hear the woodland linnet,
How sweet his music! on my life,
There's more of wisdom in it.

And hark! how blithe the throstle sings!
He, too, is no mean preacher:
Come forth into the light of things,
Let Nature be your teacher.

105

She has a world of ready wealth,
Our minds and hearts to bless –
Spontaneous wisdom breathed by health,
Truth breathed by cheerfulness.

One impulse from a vernal wood
May teach you more of man,
Of moral evil and of good,
Than all the sages can.

Sweet is the lore which Nature brings;
Our meddling intellect
Mis-shapes the beauteous forms of things: –
We murder to dissect.

Enough of Science and of Art;
Close up those barren leaves;
Come forth, and bring with you a heart
That watches and receives.

☾ 5 July · Epitaph on Sir Isaac Newton · Alexander Pope

On 5 July 1687 Sir Isaac Newton's *Philosophiae Naturalis Principia Mathematica* ('Mathematical Principles of Natural Philosophy') – regarded as one of the most important works in the history of science – was first published. The work outlines Newton's laws of motion and gravity, which are regarded as the foundation for the science of mechanics. Alexander Pope's epitaph for Newton powerfully summarizes his extraordinary contribution to science, but was not allowed to be carved into Newton's monument in Westminster Abbey.

Nature and Nature's Laws lay hid in Night.
God said, 'Let Newton be!' and All was *Light*.

☀ 6 July · Sir Isaac Newton Told Us Why · Anon.

This is another poem about Isaac Newton's theory of gravity. This comic piece comes from – of all things strange – a public information programme broadcast in the 1970s, which warned people to take care at work and to wear appropriate safety gear.

Sir Isaac Newton told us why
An apple falls down from the sky,
And from this fact, it's very plain,
All other objects do the same.
A brick, a bolt, a bar, a cup
Invariably fall down, not up,
And every common working tool
Is governed by the self-same rule.
So when you handle tools up there,
Let your watchword be 'Take Care'.
If at work you drop a spanner,
It travels in a downward manner.
At work, a fifth of accidents or more
Illustrate old Newton's law,
But one thing he forgot to add,
The damage won't be half as bad
If you are wearing proper clothes,
Especially on your head and toes.
These hats and shoes are there to save
The wearer from an early grave.
So best feet forward and take care
About the kind of shoes you wear,
It's better to be sure than dead,
So get a hat and keep your head.
Don't think to go without is brave:
The effects of gravity can be grave . . .

6 July · Rain in Summer ·
Henry Wadsworth Longfellow

Summer rain after a hot, dry spell is always welcome.
The American poet Longfellow was enchanted by it, and
catalogues the many reasons why we should welcome
it. The scope of the poem begins small, with a few
raindrops, but expands to cover heaven and earth and
the river of Time itself!

How beautiful is the rain!
After the dust and heat,
In the broad and fiery street,
In the narrow lane,
How beautiful is the rain!

How it clatters along the roofs,
Like the tramp of hoofs
How it gushes and struggles out
From the throat of the overflowing spout!

Across the window-pane
It pours and pours;
And swift and wide,
With a muddy tide,
Like a river down the gutter roars
The rain, the welcome rain!

The sick man from his chamber looks
At the twisted brooks;
He can feel the cool

Breath of each little pool;
His fevered brain
Grows calm again,
And he breathes a blessing on the rain.
From the neighboring school
Come the boys,
With more than their wonted noise
And commotion;
And down the wet streets
Sail their mimic fleets,
Till the treacherous pool
Ingulfs them in its whirling
And turbulent ocean.

In the country, on every side,
Where far and wide,
Like a leopard's tawny and spotted hide,
Stretches the plain,
To the dry grass and the drier grain
How welcome is the rain!

In the furrowed land
The toilsome and patient oxen stand;
Lifting the yoke encumbered head,
With their dilated nostrils spread,
They silently inhale
The clover-scented gale,
And the vapors that arise
From the well-watered and smoking soil.
For this rest in the furrow after toil
Their large and lustrous eyes
Seem to thank the Lord,
More than man's spoken word.

Near at hand,
From under the sheltering trees,
The farmer sees
His pastures, and his fields of grain,
As they bend their tops
To the numberless beating drops
Of the incessant rain.
He counts it as no sin
That he sees therein
Only his own thrift and gain.

These, and far more than these,
The Poet sees!
He can behold
Aquarius old
Walking the fenceless fields of air;
And from each ample fold
Of the clouds about him rolled
Scattering everywhere
The showery rain,
As the farmer scatters his grain.

He can behold
Things manifold
That have not yet been wholly told,–
Have not been wholly sung nor said.
For his thought, that never stops,
Follows the water-drops
Down to the graves of the dead,
Down through chasms and gulfs profound,
To the dreary fountain-head
Of lakes and rivers under ground;
And sees them, when the rain is done,
On the bridge of colors seven

Climbing up once more to heaven,
Opposite the setting sun.

Thus the Seer,
With vision clear,
Sees forms appear and disappear,
In the perpetual round of strange,
Mysterious change
From birth to death, from death to birth,
From earth to heaven, from heaven to earth;
Till glimpses more sublime
Of things, unseen before,
Unto his wondering eyes reveal
The Universe, as an immeasurable wheel
Turning forevermore
In the rapid and rushing river of Time.

7 July · Checking Out Me History ·
John Agard

On 7 July 1801, Toussaint Louverture became governor-general of Saint-Domingue (later renamed Haiti), having successfully led the enslaved people of the island to freedom. Agard's poem is about Louverture, but it is also about the fact that the history of marginalized people has largely gone untaught in British schools.

Dem tell me
Dem tell me
Wha dem want to tell me

Bandage up me eye with me own history
Blind me to me own identity

Dem tell me bout 1066 and all dat
dem tell me bout Dick Whittington and he cat
But Toussaint L'Ouverture
no dem never tell me bout dat

> *Toussaint*
> *a slave*
> *with vision*
> *lick back*
> *Napoleon*
> *battalion*
> *and first Black*
> *Republic born*
> *Toussaint de thorn*

to de French
Toussaint de beacon
of de Haitian Revolution

Dem tell me bout de man who discover de balloon
and de cow who jump over de moon
Dem tell me bout de dish ran away with de spoon
But dem never tell me bout Nanny de maroon

Nanny
see-far woman
of mountain dream
fire-woman struggle
hopeful stream
to freedom river

Dem tell me bout Lord Nelson and Waterloo
but dem never tell me bout Shaka de great Zulu
Dem tell me bout Columbus and 1492
but what happen to de Caribs and de Arawaks too

Dem tell me bout Florence Nightingale and she lamp
and how Robin Hood used to camp
Dem tell me bout ole King Cole was a merry ole soul
but dem never tell me bout Mary Seacole

From Jamaica
she travel far
to the Crimean War
she volunteer to go
and even when de British said no
she still brave the Russian snow
a healing star
among the wounded
a yellow sunrise
to the dying

Dem tell me
Dem tell me wha dem want to tell me
But now I checking out me own history
I carving out me identity

☾ 7 July · *from* The Pied Piper of Hamelin · Robert Browning

'The Pied Piper of Hamelin' tells the story of a mysterious man who arrived in the German city of Hamelin some time during the Middle Ages carrying a magic pipe. The city was overrun with rats, and the piper made a deal with the mayor: for a fee, he agreed to enchant the rats with his pipe and lead them into a nearby river. The piper carried out his half of the bargain, but the mayor refused to pay, whereupon the piper used his magic pipe to abduct the children of the town. The moral of the story is simple: if you've made a promise, keep it.

> Into the street the Piper stept,
>   Smiling first a little smile,
> As if he knew what magic slept
>   In his quiet pipe the while;
> Then, like a musical adept,
> To blow the pipe his lips he wrinkled,
> And green and blue his sharp eyes twinkled,
> Like a candle-flame were salt is sprinkled;
> And ere three shrill notes the pipe uttered,
> You heard as if an army muttered;
> And the muttering grew to a grumbling;
> And the grumbling grew to a mighty rumbling;
> And out of the houses the rats came tumbling.
> Great rats, small rats, lean rats, brawny rats,
> Brown rats, black rats, grey rats, tawny rats,
> Grave old plodders, gay young friskers,

Fathers, mothers, uncles, cousins,
Cocking tails and pricking whiskers,
    Families by tens and dozens,
Brothers, sisters, husbands, wives –
Followed the Piper for their lives.
From street to street he piped advancing,
And step for step they followed dancing,
Until they came to the river Weser,
    Wherein all plunged and perished!
– Save one who, stout as Julius Caesar,
Swam across and lived to carry
    (As he, the manuscript he cherished)
To Rat-land home his commentary:
Which was, 'At the first shrill notes of the pipe,
I heard a sound as of scraping tripe,
And putting apples, wondrous ripe,
Into a cider-press's gripe:
And a moving away of pickle-tub-boards,
And a leaving ajar of conserve-cupboards,
And a drawing the corks of train-oil-flasks,
And a breaking the hoops of butter-casks;
And it seemed as if a voice
    (Sweeter far than by harp or by psaltery
Is breathed) called out, 'Oh rats, rejoice!
    The world is grown to one vast drysaltery!
So munch on, crunch on, take your nuncheon,
Breakfast, supper, dinner, luncheon!'
And just as a bulky sugar-puncheon,
All ready staved, like a great sun shone
Glorious scarce an inch before me,
Just as methought it said, 'Come, bore me!'
– I found the Weser rolling o'er me.'

Walt Whitman was associated with the philosophical
movement of Transcendentalism, which believed that
people were by nature born good. This poem illustrates
Whitman's desire to see a spiritual goodness at work in
everyday experiences, where anything and everything
can start to seem miraculous.

Why, who makes much of a miracle?
As to me I know of nothing else but miracles,
Whether I walk the streets of Manhattan,
Or dart my sight over the roofs of houses toward the
    sky,
Or wade with naked feet along the beach just in the edge
    of the water,
Or stand under trees in the woods,
Or talk by day with any one I love, or sleep in the bed at
    night with any one I love,
Or sit at table at dinner with the rest,
Or look at strangers opposite me riding in the car,
Or watch honey-bees busy around the hive of a summer
    forenoon,
Or animals feeding in the fields,
Or birds, or the wonderfulness of insects in the air,
Or the wonderfulness of the sundown, or of stars
    shining so quiet and bright,
Or the exquisite delicate thin curve of the new moon in
    spring;
These with the rest, one and all, are to me miracles,
The whole referring, yet each distinct and in its place.

To me every hour of the light and dark is a miracle,
Every cubic inch of space is a miracle,
Every square yard of the surface of the earth is spread
    with the same,
Every foot of the interior swarms with the same.

To me the sea is a continual miracle,
The fishes that swim – the rocks – the motion of the
    waves – the ships with men in them,
What stranger miracles are there?

While John Keats is now remembered as one of
the greatest of English poets, when his long poem
Endymion was first published in 1818 it was met with
scathing reviews. Keats reacted in a letter to a friend:
'I was never afraid of failure; for I would sooner fail
than not be among the greatest.' The elegant opening
lines of the poem, with their comforting message of the
immortal nature of beauty, are some of Keats's most
famous words.

A thing of beauty is a joy for ever:
Its loveliness increases; it will never
Pass into nothingness; but still will keep
A bower quiet for us, and a sleep
Full of sweet dreams, and health, and quiet breathing.
Therefore, on every morrow, are we wreathing
A flowery band to bind us to the earth,
Spite of despondence, of the inhuman dearth
Of noble natures, of the gloomy days,
Of all the unhealthy and o'er-darkened ways
Made for our searching: yes, in spite of all,
Some shape of beauty moves away the pall
From our dark spirits. Such the sun, the moon,
Trees old, and young, sprouting a shady boon
For simple sheep; and such are daffodils
With the green world they live in; and clear rills
That for themselves a cooling covert make
'Gainst the hot season; the mid forest brake,

Rich with a sprinkling of fair musk-rose blooms:
And such too is the grandeur of the dooms
We have imagined for the mighty dead;
All lovely tales that we have heard or read:
An endless fountain of immortal drink,
Pouring unto us from the heaven's brink.

Edna St Vincent Millay was a celebrated American poet and a feminist activist, living in the first half of the twentieth century. This short lyric, arranged into three rhyming quatrains, expresses the writer's *wanderlust* – the desire to travel far and wide.

The railroad track is miles away,
    And the day is loud with voices speaking,
Yet there isn't a train goes by all day
    But I hear its whistle shrieking.

All night there isn't a train goes by,
    Though the night is still for sleep and dreaming,
But I see its cinders red on the sky,
    And hear its engine steaming.

My heart is warm with the friends I make,
    And better friends I'll not be knowing;
Yet there isn't a train I wouldn't take,
    No matter where it's going.

☾ 9 July · A Boat, Beneath a Sunny Sky · Lewis Carroll

Lewis Carroll is best known for his wonderful and surreal children's book *Alice in Wonderland*, which came about after he was asked to tell a story to a young girl called Alice Pleasance Liddell. This poem was also inspired by Alice, and takes the form of an 'acrostic' – read vertically, the first letters of each line combine to spell her name. The final lines echo the strange, ethereal nature of Carroll's books set in Wonderland.

> A boat, beneath a sunny sky,
> Lingering onward dreamily
> In an evening of July –
>
> Children three that nestle near,
> Eager eye and willing ear,
> Pleased a simple tale to hear –
>
> Long has paled that sunny sky:
> Echoes fade and memories die:
> Autumn frosts have slain July.
>
> Still she haunts me, phantomwise,
> Alice moving under skies
> Never seen by waking eyes.
>
> Children yet, the tale to hear,
> Eager eye and willing ear,
> Lovingly shall nestle near.

In a Wonderland they lie,
Dreaming as the days go by,
Dreaming as the summers die:

Ever drifting down the stream –
Lingering in the golden gleam –
Life, what is it but a dream?

10 July · The Magic of the Mind · Clive Webster

In Edna St Vincent Millay's poem yesterday, the narrator wanted to travel far away. This poem by Clive Webster is about the power of books and the imagination to make those journeys for us.

I've read in books of magic lands
So very far away,
Where genies pop up out of lamps
And magic creatures play.
Where wizards weave their magic spells
And dragons breathe out fire,
Where just one wish gives young and old
Their every heart's desire.

Those lands, of course, are just in books,
But if you try real hard,
Those magic places come to life
Right in your own back yard.
For sitting quietly in the sun
On a lazy Summer's day
You can sit and smile and dream you're there
In those lands so far away.

And as the sunshine warms your mind
You're in those golden lands,
With wizards, genies, dragons, spells,
And cut-throat pirate bands.
You're saving damsels in distress,
You're fighting deadly duels,
You're banqueting in marbled halls,
You're decked in priceless jewels.

You're there, you're there, no need for books,
So real and oh so clear,
So marvellous and so magical,
To touch and smell and hear,
just sitting there in golden sun
You leave your cares behind,
And go to magic places
In the Magic of your Mind.

What would you do if you suspected that someone you completely trusted had stolen one of your most prized possessions?

The Puzzler was summoned by a Queen from far away . . .
He set off as the moon came up, and journeyed night
    and day.
Then after seven suns had set, and stars lit up the sky,
He spied the golden palace on a mountainside nearby.

His advent being heralded by trumpet and by drum,
The Queen swept from her bedchamber to see just who
    had come.
The Puzzler then learned about the reason for her grief . . .
That somewhere in the palace lurked a liar and a thief.

The Queen explained some time ago she'd started to prepare
For a banquet in the palace grounds – a truly grand affair;
She'd put her gown out on the chair, then looked for
    jewels to match,
But when she'd fetched her silver box she'd seen the
    broken catch . . .
And opening the casket lid she'd found, to her dismay,
The necklace she had hoped to wear had clearly gone
    astray.

The Puzzler assured The Queen that he would do his best –
Until he'd found the wrongdoer, he swore he wouldn't rest.

127

And so he asked Her Majesty just where the jewels were
  kept . . .
She whispered that she hid them in the bed in which she
  slept.
The only other people who had known this hiding place?
Her two devoted maid servants, Penelope and Grace.
The loyalty of both these maids had won them great
  acclaim,
Her Majesty was sure though, one of them *must* be to
  blame.
But each proclaimed her innocence, and so, as he'd
  foreseen,
His task was to establish *who* had stolen from The Queen.

The Puzzler delved in his bag, and found his box of tricks.
He rummaged deep inside it then pulled out his magic
  sticks . . .
Explained the sticks had powers to detect when lies
  were told,
And thus by daybreak he was sure the story would unfold.
The maidservants, escorted by The Puzzler and guard,
Were then dismissed to spend the night in two rooms
  off the yard,
Each girl received a magic stick, identical in size,
And each was told the stick would grow if they'd been
  telling lies . . .

And when the sun rose in the sky, the maids were both
  brought out –
The Puzzler had advised The Queen that soon, without a
  doubt,
They'd know for sure *which* girl it was who'd whisked
  the jewels away . . .
He asked the girls to lay their sticks together on the clay.

And so at once Penelope put *her* stick on the ground
And as Grace placed hers next to it you couldn't hear a
    sound.
The Puzzler just pointed and declared he'd solved the case:
'I think you'll find, Your Majesty, the culprit here is Grace.'

Well, Grace at once began to wail and said it wasn't true –
Her stick was not the *longer*, but the *shorter* of the two!
The Puzzler just smiled as he put the sticks away
And everybody craned their necks to catch what he
    would say . . .

'I told each maid their stick would grow if they'd not
    told the truth,
But they're not really *magic*, they are just bits of wood,
    forsooth.
Well, as young Grace has pointed out, her stick *is*
    shorter now,
But this can only mean that it has been cut down
    somehow . . .
For thinking that her stick would grow, Grace panicked
    and took fright
And found a knife to shorten it at some time in the night,
By doing this she hoped her friend would therefore get
    the blame . . .
But we all here are witnesses to her deceit and shame.'

The Queen turned to The Puzzler and thanked him from
    her heart –
He'd used his ingenuity and talent from the start,
And as he bowed and turned away to face the rising sun,
He said, 'It's time to take my leave, my puzzling is done.'

129

11 July 1804 was the date of the notorious duel between American politicians Aaron Burr and Alexander Hamilton. Burr was then Vice President of the United States; Hamilton was Secretary of the Treasury. Their rivalry was fierce and famous, and, after a series of public exchanges, Burr challenged Hamilton to an 'affair of honour' – pistols at dawn. Burr killed Hamilton and was charged with murder, though the charges were later dropped. Eugene Field's duel is an altogether more humorous affair: through gossip told by household objects, the story is narrated of a great fight between a cat and a dog.

The gingham dog and the calico cat
Side by side on the table sat;
'T was half-past twelve, and (what do you think!)
Nor one nor t' other had slept a wink!
    The old Dutch clock and the Chinese plate
    Appeared to know as sure as fate
There was going to be a terrible spat.
        (*I wasn't there; I simply state*
        What was told to me by the Chinese plate!)

The gingham dog went 'Bow-wow-wow!'
And the calico cat replied 'Mee-ow!'
The air was littered, an hour or so,
With bits of gingham and calico,
    While the old Dutch clock in the chimney-place
    Up with its hands before its face,
For it always dreaded a family row!
        (*Now mind: I'm only telling you*
        What the old Dutch clock declares is true!)

The Chinese plate looked very blue,
And wailed, 'Oh, dear! what shall we do!'
But the gingham dog and the calico cat
Wallowed this way and tumbled that,
    Employing every tooth and claw
    In the awfullest way you ever saw –
And, oh! how the gingham and calico flew!
      (Don't fancy I exaggerate –
      I got my news from the Chinese plate!)

Next morning, where the two had sat
They found no trace of dog or cat;
And some folks think unto this day
That burglars stole that pair away!
    But the truth about the cat and pup
    Is this: they ate each other up!
Now what do you really think of that!
      (The old Dutch clock it told me so,
      And that is how I came to know.)

11 July · The Pig · Roald Dahl

In this rather gruesome poem, Roald Dahl turns the tables on bacon-chomping humans, as the clever pig of the title decides to take defensive action against being turned into sausages. Dahl doesn't shy away from detailed descriptions, whether they're funny, like the pig leaping up 'like a ballet dancer', or sinister, as the pig enjoys his unusual meal.

In England once there lived a big
And wonderfully clever pig.
To everybody it was plain
That Piggy had a massive brain.
He worked out sums inside his head,
There was no book he hadn't read.
He knew what made an airplane fly,
He knew how engines worked and why.
He knew all this, but in the end
One question drove him round the bend: He
 simply couldn't puzzle out
What LIFE was really all about.
What was the reason for his birth?
Why was he placed upon this earth?
His giant brain went round and round.
Alas, no answer could be found,
Till suddenly one wondrous night
All in a flash he saw the light.
He jumped up like a ballet dancer
And yelled, 'By gum, I've got the answer!
They want my bacon, slice by slice,
To sell at a tremendous price!
They want my tender juicy chops
To put in all the butchers' shops!

They want my pork to make a roast
And that's the part'll cost the most!
They want my sausages in strings!
They even want my chitterlings!
The butcher's shop! The carving knife!
That is the reason for my life!'
Such thoughts as these are not designed
To give a pig great peace of mind.
Next morning, in comes Farmer Bland,
A pail of pigswill in his hand,
And Piggy, with a mighty roar,
Bashes the farmer to the floor. . .
Now comes the rather grizzly bit
So let's not make too much of it,
Except that you must understand
That Piggy did eat Farmer Bland.
He ate him up from head to toe,
Chewing the pieces nice and slow.
It took an hour to reach the feet,
Because there was so much to eat,
And when he finished,
Pig, of course,
Felt absolutely no remorse.
Slowly he scratched his brainy head
And, with a little smile, he said,
'I had a fairly powerful hunch
That he might have me for his lunch.
And so, because I feared the worst,
I thought I'd better eat *him* first.'

12 July · Jerusalem (*from* Milton) · William Blake

On 12 July 1770, James Hargreaves applied for a patent for his invention, the spinning jenny. The device was used to manufacture cloth, and it greatly reduced the amount of work and the cost of making clothing and fabrics. Its invention was a key moment in the Industrial Revolution, and it helped change the shape of Britain. Though Blake did write a very long poem called 'Jerusalem', his famous 'Jerusalem Hymn', sung to music at the Last Night of the Proms, is actually from the older poem 'Milton'. Blake is well known for his worries about industrial progress, captured in the image of the 'dark Satanic Mills' of the poem.

> And did those feet in ancient time
> Walk upon England's mountains green?
> And was the holy Lamb of God,
> On England's pleasant pastures seen?
>
> And did the Countenance Divine,
> Shine forth upon our clouded hills?
> And was Jerusalem builded here
> Among those dark Satanic Mills?
>
> Bring me my Bow of burning gold:
> Bring me my Arrows of desire:
> Bring me my Spear: O clouds unfold!
> Bring me my Chariot of fire.

I will not cease from Mental Fight,
Nor shall my Sword sleep in my hand
Till we have built Jerusalem
In England's green & pleasant Land.

In this poem Robert Graves uses a technique almost like that of a dialogue to personify the moon.

The cruel Moon hangs out of reach
Up above the shadowy beech.
Her face is stupid, but her eye
Is small and sharp and very sly.
Nurse says the Moon can drive you mad?
No, that's a silly story, lad!
Though she be angry, though she would
Destroy all England if she could,
Yet think, what damage can she do
Hanging there so far from you?
Don't heed what frightened nurses say:
Moons hang much too far away.

13 July · The Argument of His Book · Robert Herrick

Herrick uses the word 'argument' in the title of this poem in its older sense, meaning the theme of the work. The 'theme' is poetry itself, and the narrator sings and composes about some of the traditional themes of lyric poetry. The 'court of Mab' refers to Queen Mab, a popular fairy figure who was first referred to by Shakespeare in *Romeo and Juliet*.

I sing of brooks, of blossoms, birds, and bowers,
Of April, May, of June, and July flowers.
I sing of May-poles, hock-carts, wassails, wakes,
Of bridegrooms, brides, and of their bridal-cakes.
I write of youth, of love, and have access
By these to sing of cleanly wantonness.
I sing of dews, of rains, and piece by piece
Of balm, of oil, of spice, and ambergris.
I sing of Time's trans-shifting; and I write
How roses first came red, and lilies white.
I write of groves, of twilights, and I sing
The court of Mab, and of the fairy king.
I write of Hell; I sing (and ever shall)
Of Heaven, and hope to have it after all.

☾ 13 July · Calendar of Sonnets: July · Helen Hunt Jackson

The nineteenth-century American poet Helen Hunt Jackson had the wonderful idea to create a sonnet cycle of twelve poems – one devoted to each month of the year – that served as a literary calendar. This July entry evokes the punishing heat that can make us all as 'weak and spent' as garden flowers in the height of summer. In these clammy, uncomfortable days we could do a lot worse than take inspiration from the stoic, regal lily, which Jackson describes floating along placidly and unperturbed in cool waters.

Some flowers are withered and some joys have died;
The garden reeks with an East Indian scent
From beds where gillyflowers stand weak and spent;
The white heat pales the skies from side to side;
But in still lakes and rivers, cool, content,
Like starry blooms on a new firmament,
White lilies float and regally abide.
In vain the cruel skies their hot rays shed;
The lily does not feel their brazen glare.
In vain the pallid clouds refuse to share
Their dews; the lily feels no thirst, no dread.
Unharmed she lifts her queenly face and head;
She drinks of living waters and keeps fair.

14 July · *from* La Marseillaise · Claude-Joseph Rouget de Lisle

14 July is Bastille Day, commemorating the storming of the Bastille fortress in Paris on this date in 1789 – one of the most significant events of the French Revolution. 'La Marseillaise' is the French national anthem. Nowadays, the anthem is sung at international sporting events and other occasions, expressing the enduring national pride of France.

Allons, enfants de la Patrie
Le jour de gloire est arrivé!
Contre nous, de la tyrannie
L'étendard sanglant est levé
Entendez-vous dans les campagnes
Mugir ces féroces soldats?
Ils viennent jusque dans nos bras
Égorger nos fils, nos compagnes!

Aux armes, citoyens!
Formez vos bataillons
Marchons, marchons!
Qu'un sang impur
Abreuve nos sillons!

139

English translation:

Arise, children of the Fatherland
The day of glory has arrived
Against us tyranny's
Bloody banner is raised
Do you hear, in the countryside
The roar of those ferocious soldiers?
They're coming right into your arms
To cut the throats of your sons, your women!

To arms, citizens!
Form your battalions
Let's march, let's march
Let an impure blood
Water our furrows!

Keats's ballad, the title of which means 'The Beautiful
Lady without Mercy', is a supernatural tale of an
ill-fated romance. Who is the mysterious wild-eyed
woman whom our lovelorn narrator finds strangely,
and rather suspiciously roaming around the fields?
Is she an uncanny iteration of the *femme fatale* – an
archetypal stock character who has brought about the
demise of countless men throughout the history of
storytelling? Perhaps she is an embodiment of Death
itself. The brilliant ambiguity of Keats's verse means
we're still asking questions two centuries on from when
it was written. The eeriness of the fable, meanwhile,
is somewhat offset by the vivid and abundant natural
imagery that runs throughout.

O what can ail thee, knight-at-arms,
    Alone and palely loitering?
The sedge has withered from the lake,
    And no birds sing.

O what can ail thee, knight-at-arms,
    So haggard and so woe-begone?
The squirrel's granary is full,
    And the harvest's done.

I see a lily on thy brow,
    With anguish moist and fever-dew,
And on thy cheeks a fading rose
    Fast withereth too.

I met a lady in the meads,
	Full beautiful – a faery's child,
Her hair was long, her foot was light,
	And her eyes were wild.

I made a garland for her head,
	And bracelets too, and fragrant zone;
She looked at me as she did love,
	And made sweet moan

I set her on my pacing steed,
	And nothing else saw all day long,
For sidelong would she bend, and sing
	A faery's song.

She found me roots of relish sweet,
	And honey wild, and manna-dew,
And sure in language strange she said –
	'I love thee true.'

She took me to her Elfin grot,
	And there she wept and sighed full sore,
And there I shut her wild wild eyes
	With kisses four.

And there she lullèd me asleep,
	And there I dreamed – Ah! woe betide! –
The latest dream I ever dreamt
	On the cold hill side.

I saw pale kings and princes too,
	Pale warriors, death-pale were they all;
They cried – 'La Belle Dame sans Merci
	Thee hath in thrall!'

I saw their starved lips in the gloam,
    With horrid warning gapèd wide,
And I awoke and found me here,
    On the cold hill's side.

And this is why I sojourn here,
    Alone and palely loitering,
Though the sedge is withered from the lake,
    And no birds sing.

☾ 15 July · Seven Times One: Exultation · Jean Ingelow

Jean Ingelow was a Victorian poet, extremely popular in her day. 'Exultation', about a child's seventh birthday, is the first in a series of lifetime poems by Ingelow that chart every seven years of a life; the others are themed around 'romance' at fourteen, 'love' at twenty-one, and, at the age of forty-nine, 'longing for home'.

There's no dew left on the daisies and clover,
    There's no rain left in heaven:
I've said my 'seven times' over and over,
    Seven times one are seven.

I am old, so old, I can write a letter;
    My birthday lessons are done;
The lambs play always, they know no better;
    They are only one times one.

O moon! in the night I have seen you sailing
    And shining so round and low.
You were bright! ah bright! but your light is failing –
    You are nothing now but a bow.

You moon! have you done something wrong in heaven
    That God has hidden your face?
I hope if you have you will soon be forgiven,
    And shine again in your place.

O velvet bee, you 're a dusty fellow,
  You've powdered your legs with gold!
O brave marsh marybuds, rich and yellow,
  Give me your money to hold!
O columbine, open your folded wrapper,
  Where two twin turtle-doves dwell!
O cuckoopint, toll me the purple clapper
  That hangs in your clear green bell!

And show me your nest with the young ones in it;
  I will not steal them away;
I am old! you may trust me, linnet, linnet –
  I am seven times one today.

☽ **15 July** · Come to the Edge ·
Christopher Logue

In 1969, Christopher Logue created this as a 'poster poem', which was displayed to advertise a show on the innovative avant-garde French poet Guillaume Apollinaire, a man he admired for his daring.

> Come to the edge.
> We might fall.
> Come to the edge.
> It's too high!
> COME TO THE EDGE!
> And they came,
> And he pushed,
> And they flew.

16 July · Particle Poems: 3 · Edwin Morgan

On 16 July 1885, after ten days of treatment, the French scientist Louis Pasteur successfully inoculated a child against rabies for the first time. The principles of vaccination that Pasteur developed have saved countless lives – millions would be a conservative estimate. Edwin Morgan's poem is a celebration of the apparently mystical principles upon which scientific discoveries are built.

Three particles lived in mystical union.
They made knife, fork, and spoon,
and earth, sea, and sky.
They made animal, vegetable, and mineral,
and faith, hope, and charity.
They made stop, caution, go,
and hickory, dickory, dock.
They made yolk, white, and shell,
and hook, line, and sinker.
They made pounds, shillings, and pence,
and Goneril, Regan, and Cordelia.
They made Shadrach, Meshach, and Abednego,
and game, set, and match.

A wandering particle captured one of them,
and the two that were left made day and night,
and left and right, and right and wrong,
and black and white, and off and on,
but things were never quite the same,
and two will always yearn for three.
They're after you, or me.

147

This extract from the ancient Norse *Njal's Saga* makes use of a very old form of poetic language: the kenning. A kenning is usually comprised of two seemingly unrelated words connected to form a new idea – or to discuss an old idea in a new way! For instance, a very ancient kenning is 'world-candle', meaning sun. We still use some kennings in modern language, however, such as describing a toddler as a 'rug-rat', or someone who loves nature as a 'tree-hugger'.

The killer of the giant's offspring
broke the strong bison of the gull's meadow.
So the gods, while the keeper of the bell despaired,
   destroyed the seashore's hawk.
The horse that rides the reefs
found no help in the King of the Greeks.

Meaning:
Thor
broke the ship.
So the gods, while the Christian priest despaired,
   destroyed the ship.
The ship
found no help in Jesus.

17 July · The School Boy · William Blake

Blake's collection of poems *Songs of Innocence and Experience* is celebrated as a great experiment in poetry, where he offsets the plain songs of joy of 'Innocence' with the complicated reflections found in 'Experience'. Here is one of Blake's *Songs of Innocence*, a song about enjoying the summer of our lives. Blake's schoolboy asks why we must turn over our 'spring' years to dull education, wasting our finest, and finite, days of our youth.

I love to rise in a summer morn
When the birds sing on every tree;
The distant huntsman winds his horn,
And the sky-lark sings with me.
O! what sweet company.

But to go to school in a summer morn,
O! it drives all joy away;
Under a cruel eye outworn,
The little ones spend the day
In sighing and dismay.

Ah! then at times I drooping sit,
And spend many an anxious hour,
Nor in my book can I take delight,
Nor sit in learning's bower,
Worn thro' with the dreary shower.

How can the bird that is born for joy
Sit in a cage and sing?
How can a child, when fears annoy,
But droop his tender wing,
And forget his youthful spring?

O! father & mother, if buds are nip'd
And blossoms blown away,
And if the tender plants are strip'd
Of their joy in the springing day,
By sorrow and care's dismay,

How shall the summer arise in joy,
Or the summer fruits appear?
Or how shall we gather what griefs destroy,
Or bless the mellowing year,
When the blasts of winter appear?

17 July · She Walks in Beauty · George Gordon, Lord Byron

This seemingly romantic panegyric is often mistakenly thought to have been written by Byron in tribute to his beloved. In fact, the poem's subject was his cousin's wife, Anne Wilmot, whose striking appearance at a party one night inspired the poet to compose this, perhaps his most quoted work. Here, he presents the woman as being similar to, and entirely in symbiosis with, the beauties of the natural world. And although Lord Byron's life was notoriously full of debauchery, he, like the pious Blake, was able to identify the virtue of innocence when he came across it.

She walks in beauty, like the night
  Of cloudless climes and starry skies;
And all that's best of dark and bright
  Meet in her aspect and her eyes:
Thus mellowed to that tender light
  Which heaven to gaudy day denies.

One shade the more, one ray the less,
  Had half impaired the nameless grace
Which waves in every raven tress,
  Or softly lightens o'er her face;
Where thoughts serenely sweet express,
  How pure, how dear their dwelling-place.

And on that cheek, and o'er that brow,
    So soft, so calm, yet eloquent,
The smiles that win, the tints that glow,
    But tell of days in goodness spent,
A mind at peace with all below,
    A heart whose love is innocent!

18 July · To You · Langston Hughes

Langston Hughes is remembered as a pioneer of the American 'jazz poetry' movement, which is built upon jazz-like movements in rhythm, repetitive phrasing, and the appearance of improvisation. Hughes was a key part of the New York-based Harlem Renaissance movement, in which African-American poets developed a sense of defiant racial pride into revolutionary jazz poetry. In this poem, Hughes uses dashes at the ends of lines to create a sense that he is pausing, or changing direction in his thoughts, as if he is turning over a problem in his mind.

> To sit and dream, to sit and read,
> To sit and learn about the world
> Outside our world of here and now—
>   Our problem world—
> To dream of vast horizons of the soul
> Through dreams made whole,
> Unfettered, free—help me!
> All you who are dreamers too,
>   Help me to make
>   Our world anew.
> I reach out my dreams to you.

153

This poem, written in 1875, has been quoted in speeches by Winston Churchill in 1941, and Barack Obama in 2013. Nelson Mandela, the South African freedom fighter and later President of his country, whose birthday was 18 July, allegedly found this poem a great comfort during the twenty-seven years he spent in prison. 'Invictus' is the Latin word for 'unconquered'.

Out of the night that covers me,
    Black as the pit from pole to pole,
I thank whatever gods may be
    For my unconquerable soul.

In the fell clutch of circumstance
    I have not winced nor cried aloud.
Under the bludgeonings of chance
    My head is bloody, but unbowed.

Beyond this place of wrath and tears
    Looms but the Horror of the shade,
And yet the menace of the years
    Finds and shall find me unafraid.

It matters not how strait the gate,
    How charged with punishments the scroll,
I am the master of my fate,
    I am the captain of my soul.

☀ **19 July** · *from* Julius Caesar · William Shakespeare

During his incarceration Nelson Mandela found solace in the words of one of the greatest of writers: William Shakespeare. These lines from Shakespeare's tragedy *Julius Caesar* are among those that Mandela marked as particularly significant in a copy of the Collected Works secretly kept in his prison on Robben Island.

Cowards die many times before their deaths;
The valiant never taste of death but once.
Of all the wonders that I yet have heard,
It seems to me most strange that men should fear,
Seeing that death, a necessary end,
Will come when it will come.

From the Harlem Renaissance to Harlem hopscotch. Harlem is an area in the north of Manhattan, New York, and since the mass-migration movements of 1905 it has had a largely African-American population. Alongside its vibrant cultural history, however, Harlem has another history – one of poverty and deprivation. In Angelou's poem, there is hardship and heartache, but the poem ends on a note of hope.

One foot down, then hop! It's hot.
　　　Good things for the ones that's got.
Another jump, now to the left.
　　　Everybody for hisself.

In the air, now both feet down.
　　　Since you black, don't stick around.
Food is gone, the rent is due,
　　　Curse and cry and then jump two.

All the people out of work,
　　　Hold for three, then twist and jerk.
Cross the line, they count you out.
　　　That's what hopping's all about.

Both feet flat, the game is done.
They think I lost. I think I won.

20 July · Morning Song · Sara Teasdale

On 20 July 1969, the American Apollo 11 spacecraft, carrying astronauts Neil Armstrong, Buzz Aldrin, and Michael Collins, safely landed on the moon. Armstrong became the first man to set foot on the moon's surface. This poem depicts the moon one morning, seemingly alone in the sky.

A diamond of a morning
Waked me an hour too soon;
Dawn had taken in the stars
And left the faint white moon.

O white moon, you are lonely,
It is the same with me,
But we have the world to roam over,
Only the lonely are free.

☾ 20 July • The First Men on the Moon • J. Patrick Lewis

Neil Armstrong's declaration, 'One small step for man, one giant leap for mankind', has become one of the most famous remarks in history. The two epigraphs shown below are other iconic exclamations from that historic day.

'The Eagle has landed!' —Apollo 11 Commander
Neil A. Armstrong
'A magnificent desolation!' – Air Force Colonel
Edwin E. 'Buzz' Aldrin, Jr.
July 20, 1969

That afternoon in mid-July,
Two pilgrims watched from distant space
The moon ballooning in the sky.
They rose to meet it face-to-face.

Their spidery spaceship, Eagle, dropped
Down gently on the lunar sand.
And when the module's engines stopped,
Rapt silence fell across the land.

The first man down the ladder, Neil,
Spoke words that we remember now—
'One small step . . .' It made us feel
As if we were there too, somehow.

When Neil planted the flag and Buzz
Collected lunar rocks and dust,
They hopped like kangaroos because
Of gravity. Or wanderlust?

A quarter million miles away,
One small blue planet watched in awe.
And no one who was there that day
Will soon forget the sight they saw.

21 July • Little White Lily • George MacDonald

The Scottish poet George MacDonald is less read today than he was in his own time, but he was a big influence on other writers, including his friend Lewis Carroll. Around this time of year, in the warmer months, we see the flowering of lilies.

> Little white Lily
>   Sat by a stone,
> Drooping and waiting
>   Till the sun shone.
> Little white Lily
>   Sunshine has fed;
> Little white Lily
>   Is lifting her head.
>
> Little white Lily
>   Said: 'It is good:
> Little white Lily's
>   Clothing and food!
> Little white Lily
>   Drest like a bride!
> Shining with whiteness,
>   And crownèd beside!'
>
> Little white Lily
>   Droopeth in pain,
> Waiting and waiting
>   For the wet rain.
> Little white Lily
>   Holdeth her cup;
> Rain is fast falling,
>   And filling it up.

Little white Lily
  Said: 'Good again,
When I am thirsty
  To have nice rain!
Now I am stronger,
  Now I am cool;
Heat cannot burn me,
  My veins are so full!'

Little white Lily
  Smells very sweet:
On her head sunshine,
  Rain at her feet.
'Thanks to the sunshine!
  Thanks to the rain!
Little white Lily
  Is happy again!'

Laurie Lee's autobiographical account of growing up in rural Gloucestershire is called *Cider with Rosie*, and in this poem the 'cidery bite' of the apples makes a vivid appearance.

Behold the apples' rounded worlds:
juice-green of July rain,
the black polestar of flowers, the rind
mapped with its crimson stain.

The russet, crab and cottage red
burn to the sun's hot brass,
then drop like sweat from every branch
and bubble in the grass.

They lie as wanton as they fall,
and where they fall and break,
the stallion clamps his crunching jaws,
the starling stabs his beak.

In each plump gourd the cidery bite
of boys' teeth tears the skin;
the waltzing wasp consumes his share,
the bent worm enters in.

I, with as easy hunger, take
entire my season's dole;
welcome the ripe, the sweet, the sour,
the hollow and the whole.

22 July · The Law of the Jungle · Rudyard Kipling

This poem appears in Kipling's *The Second Jungle Book*. While the phrase 'the law of the jungle' tends to mean 'survival of the fittest', here it refers to actual laws and codes of practice held by a pack of wolves.

Now this is the Law of the Jungle – as old and as true
*   as the sky;*
And the Wolf that shall keep it may prosper, but the
*   Wolf that shall break it must die.*

As the creeper that girdles the tree-trunk, the Law
*   runneth forward and back –*
For the strength of the Pack is the Wolf, and the
*   strength of the Wolf is the Pack.*

Wash daily from nose-tip to tail-tip; drink deeply, but
    never too deep;
And remember the night is for hunting, and forget not
    the day is for sleep.

The Jackal may follow the Tiger, but, Cub, when thy
    whiskers are grown,
Remember the Wolf is a hunter – go forth and get food
    of thy own.

Keep peace with the Lords of the Jungle – the Tiger, the
    Panther, the Bear;
And trouble not Hathi the Silent, and mock not the Boar
    in his lair.

163

When Pack meets with Pack in the Jungle, and neither
  will go from the trail,
Lie down till the leaders have spoken – it may be fair
  words shall prevail.

When ye fight with a Wolf of the Pack, ye must fight him
  alone and afar,
Lest others take part in the quarrel and the Pack be
  diminished by war.

The Lair of the Wolf is his refuge, and where he has
  made him his home,
Not even the Head Wolf may enter, not even the Council
  may come.

The Lair of the Wolf is his refuge, but where he has
  digged it too plain,
The Council shall send him a message, and so he shall
  change it again.

If ye kill before midnight, be silent, and wake not the
  woods with your bay,
Lest ye frighten the deer from the crops, and thy
  brothers go empty away.

Ye may kill for yourselves, and your mates, and your
  cubs as they need, and ye can;
But kill not for pleasure of killing, and *seven times
  never kill Man.*

If ye plunder his Kill from a weaker, devour not all in
  thy pride;
Pack-Right is the right of the meanest; so leave him the
  head and the hide.

164

The Kill of the Pack is the meat of the Pack. Ye must eat
    where it lies;
And no one may carry away of that meat to his lair, or
    he dies.

The Kill of the Wolf is the meat of the Wolf. He may do
    what he will,
But, till he has given permission, the Pack may not eat
    of that Kill.

Cub-Right is the right of the Yearling. From all of his
    Pack he may claim.
Full-gorge when the killer has eaten; and none may
    refuse him the same.

Lair-Right is the right of the Mother. From all of her
    year she may claim
One haunch of each kill for her litter, and none may
    deny her the same.

Cave-Right is the right of the Father – to hunt by
    himself for his own:
He is freed from all calls to the Pack; he is judged by the
    Council alone.

Because of his age and his cunning, because of his gripe
    and his paw,
In all that the law leaveth open, the word of the Head
    Wolf is Law.

Now these are the Laws of the Jungle, and many and
    mighty are they;
But the head and the hoof of the Law and the haunch
    and the hump is – Obey!

Billy Collins is a much admired American poet. This free verse poem is purposefully ambiguous, as Collins describes 'walking across' the Atlantic Ocean. It is unclear whether the poem's speaker is actually walking across the water, or just using their imagination, just as they are when they picture what their feet must look like from the perspective of the fish.

I wait for the holiday crowd to clear the beach
before stepping onto the first wave.

Soon I am walking across the Atlantic
thinking about Spain,
checking for whales, waterspouts.
I feel the water holding up my shifting weight.
Tonight I will sleep on its rocking surface.

But for now I try to imagine what
this must look like to the fish below,
the bottoms of my feet appearing, disappearing.

23 July • The Mermaid • Alfred, Lord Tennyson

This poem is one of a pair by Tennyson. Taken together, the poems of the mermaid and merman represent female and male characteristics and – because they are daydreams – human desires. And, perhaps unsurprisingly, both the mermaid and merman are extraordinarily vain!

I

Who would be
A mermaid fair,
Singing alone,
Combing her hair
Under the sea,
In a golden curl
With a comb of pearl,
On a throne?

II

I would be a mermaid fair;
I would sing to myself the whole of the day;
With a comb of pearl I would comb my hair;
And still as I comb'd I would sing and say,
'Who is it loves me? who loves not me?'
I would comb my hair till my ringlets would fall
Low adown, low adown,
From under my starry sea-bud crown
Low adown and around,

167

And I should look like a fountain of gold
     Springing alone
  With a shrill inner sound,
     Over the throne
    In the midst of the hall;
Till that great sea-snake under the sea
From his coiled sleeps in the central deeps
Would slowly trail himself sevenfold
Round the hall where I sate, and look in at the gate
With his large calm eyes for the love of me.
And all the mermen under the sea
Would feel their immortality
Die in their hearts for the love of me.

III

But at night I would wander away, away,
  I would fling on each side my low-flowing locks,
And lightly vault from the throne and play
  With the mermen in and out of the rocks;
We would run to and fro, and hide and seek,
  On the broad sea-wolds in the crimson shells,
Whose silvery spikes are nighest the sea.
But if any came near I would call and shriek,
And adown the steep like a wave I would leap
  From the diamond-ledges that jut from the dells;
For I would not be kiss'd by all who would list,
Of the bold merry mermen under the sea.
They would sue me, and woo me, and flatter me,
In the purple twilights under the sea;
But the king of them all would carry me,
Woo me, and win me, and marry me,
In the branching jaspers under the sea.

Then all the dry-pied things that be
In the hueless mosses under the sea
Would curl round my silver feet silently,
All looking up for the love of me.
And if I should carol aloud, from aloft
All things that are forked, and horned, and soft
Would lean out from the hollow sphere of the sea,
All looking down for the love of me.

Where the speaker in the first poem imagined being
a mermaid so beautiful that men forgot to think of
themselves and became slaves to her appearance, this
poem presents a masculine form of vanity: a man who
imagines himself as bold and powerful, and who kisses
mermaids until they kiss him back – he takes what he
wants, and seems unpleasant for it.

I

Who would be
A merman bold,
Sitting alone,
Singing alone
Under the sea,
With a crown of gold,
On a throne?

II

I would be a merman bold,
I would sit and sing the whole of the day;
I would fill the sea-halls with a voice of power;
But at night I would roam abroad and play
With the mermaids in and out of the rocks,
Dressing their hair with the white sea-flower;
And holding them back by their flowing locks
I would kiss them often under the sea,
And kiss them again till they kiss'd me

Laughingly, laughingly;
And then we would wander away, away,
To the pale-green sea-groves straight and high,
　Chasing each other merrily.

III

There would be neither moon nor star;
But the wave would make music above us afar –
Low thunder and light in the magic night –
　Neither moon nor star.
We would call aloud in the dreamy dells,
Call to each other and whoop and cry
　All night, merrily, merrily.
They would pelt me with starry spangles and shells,
Laughing and clapping their hands between,
　All night, merrily, merrily,
But I would throw to them back in mine
Turkis and agate and almondine;
Then leaping out upon them unseen
I would kiss them often under the sea,
And kiss them again till they kiss'd me
　Laughingly, laughingly.
O, what a happy life were mine
Under the hollow-hung ocean green!
Soft are the moss-beds under the sea;
We would live merrily, merrily.

24 July • The Shark • Lord Alfred Douglas

Lord Alfred Douglas was an English poet, author and translator. In this poem, the 'warning' that comes at the end of the shark's 'dangerous bite' contrasts with the jaunty rhythm of the piece as a whole.

A treacherous monster is the Shark
He never makes the least remark.

And when he sees you on the sand,
He doesn't seem to want to land.

He watches you take off your clothes,
And not the least excitement shows.

His eyes do not grow bright or roll,
He has astonishing self-control.

He waits till you are quite undressed,
And seems to take no interest.

And when towards the sea you leap,
He looks as if he were asleep.

But when you once get in his range,
His whole demeanour seems to change.

He throws his body right about,
And his true character comes out.

It's no use crying or appealing,
He seems to lose all decent feeling.

After this warning you will wish
To keep clear of this treacherous fish.

His back is black, his stomach white,
He has a very dangerous bite.

☾ 24 July · maggie and milly and molly and may · E. E. Cummings

E. E. Cummings wrote a great deal of very unusual-looking poetry: he used grammar and lower-case letters in unexpected ways— and sometimes he paid no attention to syntax at all! With its lack of capitalized names and strange punctuation, this poem is an example of visual verse – a type of poetry developed by Cummings that uses the physical layout of the words on a page to accentuate the poem's meaning.

maggie and milly and molly and may
went down to the beach (to play one day)

and maggie discovered a shell that sang
so sweetly she couldn't remember her troubles,and

milly befriended a stranded star
whose rays five languid fingers were;

and molly was chased by a horrible thing
which raced sideways while blowing bubbles:and

may came home with a smooth round stone
as small as a world and as large as alone.

For whatever we lose (like a you or a me)
it's always ourselves we find in the sea

174

There is nothing more summery than a trip to the seaside on a sunny day. However, Edgar Allan Poe has a reputation for dark, gothic poems, and this one is about a youthful romance cut short by the death of a young woman.

It was many and many a year ago,
   In a kingdom by the sea,
That a maiden there lived whom you may know
   By the name of Annabel Lee;
And this maiden she lived with no other thought
   Than to love and be loved by me.

She was a child and I was a child,
   In this kingdom by the sea,
But we loved with a love that was more than love –
   I and my Annabel Lee –
With a love that the wingèd seraphs of Heaven
   Coveted her and me.

And this was the reason that, long ago,
   In this kingdom by the sea,
A wind blew out of a cloud by night
   Chilling my Annabel Lee;
So that her highborn kinsmen came
   And bore her away from me,
To shut her up in a sepulchre
   In this kingdom by the sea.

The angels, not half so happy in Heaven,
    Went envying her and me:
Yes! that was the reason (as all men know,
    In this kingdom by the sea)
That the wind came out of the cloud, chilling
    And killing my Annabel Lee.

But our love it was stronger by far than the love
    Of those who were older than we –
    Of many far wiser than we –
And neither the angels in Heaven above
    Nor the demons down under the sea,
Can ever dissever my soul from the soul
    Of the beautiful Annabel Lee:

For the moon never beams without bringing me dreams
    Of the beautiful Annabel Lee;
And the stars never rise, but I feel the bright eyes
    Of the beautiful Annabel Lee;
And so, all the night-tide, I lie down by the side
Of my darling, my darling, my life and my bride,
    In her sepulchre there by the sea –
    In her tomb by the side of the sea.

🌒 **25 July** · The Night Mail · W. H. Auden

On 25 July 1814, George Stephenson demonstrated the first fully effective steam train, a milestone which was to transform travel in the nineteenth century. Auden wrote 'The Night Mail' for the 1936 documentary film of the same name, which followed the Postal Special train as it brought mail up from London as far as Aberdeen.

This is the Night Mail crossing the border,
Bringing the cheque and the postal order,
Letters for the rich, letters for the poor,
The shop at the corner and the girl next door.
Pulling up Beattock, a steady climb—
The gradient's against her, but she's on time.

Past cotton-grass and moorland boulder
Shovelling white steam over her shoulder,
Snorting noisily as she passes
Silent miles of wind-bent grasses;
Birds turn their heads as she approaches,
Stare from the bushes at her blank-faced coaches;
Sheepdogs cannot turn her course;
They slumber on with paws across,
In the farm she passes no one wakes,
But a jug in the bedroom gently shakes.

Dawn freshens, the climb is done.
Down towards Glasgow she descends
Towards the steam tugs, yelping down the glade of cranes
Towards the fields of apparatus, the furnaces
Set on the dark plain like gigantic chessmen.
All Scotland waits for her;
In the dark glens, beside the pale-green sea lochs
Men long for news.

Letters of thanks, letters from banks,
Letters of joy from the girl and boy,
Receipted bills and invitations
To inspect new stock or visit relations,
And applications for situations
And timid lovers' declarations
And gossip, gossip from all the nations;
News circumstantial, news financial,
Letters with holiday snaps to enlarge in,
Letters with faces scrawled in the margin.
Letters from uncles, cousins, and aunts,
Letters to Scotland from the South of France,
Letters of condolence to Highlands and Lowlands
Notes from overseas to Hebrides;
Written on paper of every hue,
The pink, the violet, the white and the blue
The chatty, the catty, the boring, adoring,
The cold and official and the heart's outpouring,
Clever, stupid, short and long,
The typed and the printed and the spelt all wrong.

Thousands are still asleep
Dreaming of terrifying monsters
Or friendly tea beside the band at Cranston's or
    Crawford's;
Asleep in working Glasgow, asleep in well-set Edinburgh;
Asleep in granite Aberdeen,
They continue their dreams
But shall wake soon and long for letters.
And none will hear the postman's knock
Without a quickening of the heart,
For who can bear to feel himself forgotten?

26 July · Watching My Dog Sleep · Kae Tempest

Kae Tempest's talent for focusing intently on everyday things shines forth in this poem. The narrator cannot know what the dog is really thinking or dreaming about, but by imposing his or her own concerns about the past on to the dog, the poem surprises us with the anguish of the final lines.

after Dermot Healy

Murphy is dreaming:
his muscles are twitching,
his ears are alive,
his paws scrape the air.

He's dreaming of yesterday,
stones thrown into waves.
The heartbreak of chasing
what's no longer there.

'Fern Hill' is a reminiscence of a rural childhood which tackles common poetic subjects – the passing of time, the loss of youth and innocence, and the blurring of memory.

Now as I was young and easy under the apple boughs
About the lilting house and happy as the grass was green,
    The night above the dingle starry,
        Time let me hail and climb
    Golden in the heydays of his eyes,
And honoured among wagons I was prince of the apple
    towns
And once below a time I lordly had the trees and leaves
        Trail with daisies and barley
    Down the rivers of the windfall light.

And as I was green and carefree, famous among the barns
About the happy yard and singing as the farm was home,
    In the sun that is young once only,
        Time let me play and be
    Golden in the mercy of his means,
And green and golden I was huntsman and herdsman,
    the calves
Sang to my horn, the foxes on the hills barked clear and
    cold,
        And the sabbath rang slowly
    In the pebbles of the holy streams.

All the sun long it was running, it was lovely, the hay—
Fields high as the house, the tunes from the chimneys, it
   was air
   And playing, lovely and watery
     And fire green as grass.
   And nightly under the simple stars
As I rode to sleep the owls were bearing the farm away,
All the moon long I heard, blessed among stables, the
   nightjars
   Flying with the ricks, and the horses
     Flashing into the dark.

And then to awake, and the farm, like a wanderer white
With the dew, come back, the cock on his shoulder: it
   was all
   Shining, it was Adam and maiden,
     The sky gathered again
   And the sun grew round that very day.
So it must have been after the birth of the simple light
In the first, spinning place, the spellbound horses
   walking warm
   Out of the whinnying green stable
     On to the fields of praise.

And honoured among foxes and pheasants by the gay
   house
Under the new made clouds and happy as the heart was
   long,
   In the sun born over and over,
     I ran my heedless ways,
   My wishes raced through the house-high hay
And nothing I cared, at my sky blue trades, that time
   allows
In all his tuneful turning so few and such morning songs

Before the children green and golden
      Follow him out of grace,

Nothing I cared, in the lamb white days, that time
      would take me
Up to the swallow thronged loft by the shadow of my hand,
      In the moon that is always rising,
            Nor that riding to sleep
      I should hear him fly with the high fields
And wake to the farm forever fled from the childless land.
Oh as I was young and easy in the mercy of his means,
            Time held me green and dying
      Though I sang in my chains like the sea.

In July or August falls Tisha B'Av, a period of fasting within the Jewish calendar. It commemorates several ancient tragedies, including the Babylonian conquest of Jerusalem. The lines of this 'psalm', which comes from a Greek word for lyrical music or poetry, express the grief of the Jewish people in exile.

By the rivers of Babylon, there we sat down, yea, we
    wept, when we remembered Zion.
We hanged our harps upon the willows in the midst
    thereof.
For there they that carried us away captive required
    of us a song; and they that wasted us required of us
    mirth, saying, Sing us one of the songs of Zion.
How shall we sing the Lord's song in a strange land?
If I forget thee, O Jerusalem, let my right hand forget
    her cunning.
If I do not remember thee, let my tongue cleave to the
    roof of my mouth; if I prefer not Jerusalem above my
    chief joy.
Remember, O Lord, the children of Edom in the day
    of Jerusalem; who said, Rase it, rase it, even to the
    foundation thereof.
O daughter of Babylon, who art to be destroyed; happy
    shall he be, that rewardeth thee as thou hast served
    us.

27 July · Sea Fever · John Masefield

John Masefield was a twentieth-century British poet and novelist who served as Poet Laureate of the United Kingdom. This poem describes the deep longing of its speaker to return to the sea. Even though the imagery of the 'wheels' kicking suggests that the ship in the poem is travelling during a dangerous storm, the 'wild call' and the excitement of the seafaring life is more exciting than the safety of life at home.

I must go down to the seas again, to the lonely sea and
    the sky,
And all I ask is a tall ship and a star to steer her by;
And the wheel's kick and the wind's song and the white
    sail's shaking,
And a grey mist on the sea's face, and a grey dawn breaking.

I must go down to the seas again, for the call of the
    running tide
Is a wild call and a clear call that may not be denied;
And all I ask is a windy day with the white clouds flying,
And the flung spray and the blown spume, and the sea-
    gulls crying.

I must go down to the seas again, to the vagrant gypsy
    life,
To the gull's way and the whale's way where the wind's
    like a whetted knife;
And all I ask is a merry yarn from a laughing fellow-rover,
And quiet sleep and a sweet dream when the long trick's
    over.

185

28 July · 'next to of course god america i' · E. E. Cummings

The First World War began on this date in 1914, and lasted until November 1918. The absurd tragedy of the war is unspeakable, but E. E. Cummings conveys a small sense of it through these deeply ironic lines about patriotism, in which the fallen are the 'heroic happy dead'.

'next to of course god america i
love you land of the pilgrims' and so forth oh
say can you see by the dawn's early my
country 'tis of centuries come and go
and are no more what of it we should worry
in every language even deafanddumb
thy sons acclaim your glorious name by gorry
by jingo by gee by gosh by gum
why talk of beauty what could be more beaut-
iful than these heroic happy dead
who rushed like lions to the roaring slaughter
they did not stop to think they died instead
then shall the voice of liberty be mute?'

He spoke. And drank rapidly a glass of water

'MCMXIV' is '1914' in Roman numerals – a number, and year, that will forever be associated with the start of four years of bloodshed and devastation. In this 1964 poem, Philip Larkin traces the journey of the young, achingly naive men who went to fight in the spirit of jolly camaraderie, not knowing the horrors they would face; the innocence they would irrevocably lose. The poem is a single sentence, spread over four verses in a manner perhaps enacting the miles of trenches and lines of desperate soldiers. Or perhaps even the near-endless rows of graves of fallen soldiers; indeed, the numerals may in fact be a reference to the inscriptions on their tombs.

Those long uneven lines
Standing as patiently
As if they were stretched outside
The Oval or Villa Park,
The crowns of hats, the sun
On moustached archaic faces
Grinning as if it were all
An August Bank Holiday lark;

And the shut shops, the bleached
Established names on the sunblinds,
The farthings and sovereigns,
And dark-clothed children at play
Called after kings and queens,
The tin advertisements
For cocoa and twist, and the pubs
Wide open all day;

And the countryside not caring:
The place-names all hazed over
With flowering grasses, and fields
Shadowing Domesday lines
Under wheat's restless silence;
The differently-dressed servants
With tiny rooms in huge houses,
The dust behind limousines;

Never such innocence,
Never before or since,
As changed itself to past
Without a word – the men
Leaving the gardens tidy,
The thousands of marriages,
Lasting a little while longer:
Never such innocence again.

29 July • The Dug-Out • Siegfried Sassoon

So awful were the horrors of the First World War,
that soldiers sought to express their experiences in
any way they could. For some, this meant poetry, and
Siegfried Sassoon, who fought on the Western Front, is
remembered for his powerful wartime writings.

Why do you lie with your legs ungainly huddled,
And one arm bent across your sullen, cold,
Exhausted face? It hurts my heart to watch you,
Deep-shadowed from the candle's guttering gold;
And you wonder why I shake you by the shoulder;
Drowsy, you mumble and sigh and turn your head . . .
You are too young to fall asleep for ever;
And when you sleep you remind me of the dead.

Hilda Doolittle, who published under the name H. D., was an American modernist poet – notable for her avant-garde and experimental style.

O wind, rend open the heat,
cut apart the heat,
rend it to tatters.

Fruit cannot drop
through this thick air –
fruit cannot fall into heat
that presses up and blunts
the points of pears
and rounds the grapes.

Cut the heat –
plough through it,
turning it on either side
of your path.

In this short poem, D. H. Lawrence's use of alliterative '*sw*' sounds, as he describes the movement of the seaweed, creates a vivid picture of its movements in the water (as well as compressing the word 'seaweed' itself).

> Seaweed sways and sways and swirls
> as if swaying were its form of stillness;
> and it flushes against fierce rock
> it slips over it as shadows do, without hurting itself.

🌙 30 July · The Inchcape Rock · Robert Southey

Five years after the publication of this poem in 1802, work began on the construction of a lighthouse on Inchcape, which still stands today.

No stir in the air, no stir in the sea,
The Ship was still as she could be;
Her sails from heaven received no motion,
Her keel was steady in the ocean.

Without either sign or sound of their shock,
The waves flow'd over the Inchcape Rock;
So little they rose, so little they fell,
They did not move the Inchcape Bell.

The Abbot of Aberbrothok
Had placed that bell on the Inchcape Rock;
On a buoy in the storm it floated and swung,
And over the waves its warning rung.

When the Rock was hid by the surge's swell,
The Mariners heard the warning Bell;
And then they knew the perilous Rock,
And blest the Abbot of Aberbrothok

The Sun in the heaven was shining gay,
All things were joyful on that day;
The sea-birds scream'd as they wheel'd round,
And there was joyaunce in their sound.

The buoy of the Inchcape Bell was seen
A darker speck on the ocean green;
Sir Ralph the Rover walk'd his deck,
And fix'd his eye on the darker speck.

He felt the cheering power of spring,
It made him whistle, it made him sing;
His heart was mirthful to excess,
But the Rover's mirth was wickedness.

His eye was on the Inchcape Float;
Quoth he, 'My men, put out the boat,
And row me to the Inchcape Rock,
And I'll plague the Abbot of Aberbrothok.'

The boat is lower'd, the boatmen row,
And to the Inchcape Rock they go;
Sir Ralph bent over from the boat,
And he cut the Bell from the Inchcape Float.

Down sank the Bell with a gurgling sound,
The bubbles rose and burst around;
Quoth Sir Ralph, 'The next who comes to the Rock,
Won't bless the Abbot of Aberbrothok.'

Sir Ralph the Rover sail'd away,
He scour'd the seas for many a day;
And now grown rich with plunder'd store,
He steers his course for Scotland's shore.

So thick a haze o'erspreads the sky,
They cannot see the sun on high;
The wind hath blown a gale all day,
At evening it hath died away.

On the deck the Rover takes his stand,
So dark it is they see no land.
Quoth Sir Ralph, 'It will be lighter soon,
For there is the dawn of the rising Moon.'

'Canst hear,' said one, 'the breakers roar?
For methinks we should be near the shore.'
'Now, where we are I cannot tell,
But I wish we could hear the Inchcape Bell.'

They hear no sound, the swell is strong,
Though the wind hath fallen they drift along;
Till the vessel strikes with a shivering shock,
'Oh Christ! It is the Inchcape Rock!'

Sir Ralph the Rover tore his hair,
He curst himself in his despair;
The waves rush in on every side,
The ship is sinking beneath the tide.

But even in his dying fear,
One dreadful sound could the Rover hear;
A sound as if with the Inchcape Bell,
The Devil below was ringing his knell.

31 July *from* The Rime of the Ancient Mariner • Samuel Taylor Coleridge

Coleridge's long poem 'The Rime of the Ancient Mariner' is a poetic masterpiece. It draws on archaic language and the traditional ballad form to tell the sorry story of a sailor who kills an albatross and thus curses himself and his crew to a terrible fate. The critic William Hazlitt called it 'unquestionably a work of genius – of wild, irregular, overwhelming imagination'. It has given us such famous phrases as 'water, water, everywhere, nor any drop to drink', and 'a sadder and a wiser man'.

Beyond the shadow of the ship,
I watched the water-snakes:
They moved in tracks of shining white,
And when they reared, the elfish light
Fell off in hoary flakes.

Within the shadow of the ship
I watched their rich attire:
Blue, glossy green, and velvet black,
They coiled and swam; and every track
Was a flash of golden fire.

O happy living things! no tongue
Their beauty might declare:
A spring of love gushed from my heart,
And I blessed them unaware:
Sure my kind saint took pity on me,
And I blessed them unaware.

It is thought that Rudyard Kipling was inspired to write this poem by hearing stories of smugglers during a stay in Cornwall.

If you wake at midnight, and hear a horse's feet,
Don't go drawing back the blind, or looking in the street,
Them that ask no questions isn't told a lie.
Watch the wall my darling while the Gentlemen go by!
Five and twenty ponies,
Trotting through the dark –
Brandy for the Parson,
'Baccy for the Clerk;
Laces for a lady; letters for a spy,
And watch the wall, my darling, while the Gentlemen go
    by!
Running round the woodlump if you chance to find
Little barrels, roped and tarred, all full of brandy-wine,
Don't you shout to come and look, nor use 'em for your
    play.
Put the brishwood back again – and they'll be gone next
    day!

If you see the stable-door setting open wide;
If you see a tired horse lying down inside;
If your mother mends a coat cut about and tore;
If the lining's wet and warm – don't you ask no more!

If you meet King George's men, dressed in blue and red,
You be careful what you say, and mindful what is said.
If they call you 'pretty maid', and chuck you 'neath the
    chin,
Don't you tell where no one is, nor yet where no one's
    been!

Knocks and footsteps round the house – whistles after
    dark –
You've no call for running out till the house-dogs bark.
Trusty's here, and *Pincher*'s here, and see how dumb
    they lie –
They don't fret to follow when the Gentlemen go by!

If you do as you've been told, likely there's a chance,
You'll be give a dainty doll, all the way from France,
With a cap of Valenciennes, and a velvet hood –
A present from the Gentlemen, along 'o being good!
Five and twenty ponies,
Trotting through the dark –
Brandy for the Parson,
'Baccy for the Clerk.
Them that asks no questions isn't told a lie –
Watch the wall, my darling, while the Gentlemen go by!

August

1 August · Casabianca · Felicia Hemans

The Battle of the Nile, between the British Navy and Napoleon's French Navy, took place on 1–3 August 1798. The poet Felicia Hemans is not as well known today as she was during her lifetime in the early nineteenth century, but the first line of this poem has become very famous indeed! This much-copied, much-parodied line actually describes a real scene from the Battle of the Nile. Hemans wrote this note explaining the poem: 'Young Casabianca, a boy about thirteen years old, son to the Admiral of the Orient, remained at his post (in the Battle of the Nile) after the ship had taken fire, and all the guns had been abandoned; and perished in the explosion of the vessel, when the flames had reached the powder.'

> The boy stood on the burning deck
>   Whence all but he had fled;
> The flame that lit the battle's wreck
>   Shone round him o'er the dead.
>
> Yet beautiful and bright he stood,
>   As born to rule the storm –
> A creature of heroic blood,
>   A proud, though child-like form.
>
> The flames rolled on – he would not go
>   Without his father's word;
> That father, faint in death below,
>   His voice no longer heard.

He called aloud – 'Say, Father, say
    If yet my task is done!'
He knew not that the chieftain lay
    Unconscious of his son.

'Speak, Father!' once again he cried,
    'If I may yet be gone!'
And but the booming shots replied,
    And fast the flames rolled on.

Upon his brow he felt their breath,
    And in his waving hair,
And looked from that lone post of death
    In still yet brave despair;

And shouted but once more aloud,
    'My father! must I stay?'
While o'er him fast, through sail and shroud,
    The wreathing fires made way.

They wrapt the ship in splendour wild,
    They caught the flag on high,
And streamed above the gallant child,
    Like banners in the sky.

There came a burst of thunder sound –
    The boy – oh! where was he?
Ask of the winds that far around
    With fragments strewed the sea! –

With mast, and helm, and pennon fair,
    That well had borne their part;
But the noblest thing which perished there
    Was that young faithful heart!

1 August · Silver · Walter de la Mare

Have you ever been for a walk at night and noticed how things seem to look very different from how they do in the daytime? In this poem, Walter de la Mare describes a different kind of walk, as he imagines the moon herself walking across the landscape, changing everything she sees by casting it in her silvery light.

Slowly, silently, now the moon
Walks the night in her silver shoon;
This way, and that, she peers, and sees
Silver fruit upon silver trees;
One by one the casements catch
Her beams beneath the silvery thatch;
Couched in his kennel, like a log,
With paws of silver sleeps the dog;
From their shadowy cote the white breasts peep
Of doves in silver feathered sleep
A harvest mouse goes scampering by,
With silver claws, and silver eye;
And moveless fish in the water gleam,
By silver reeds in a silver stream.

201

2 August · Casabianca (A Parody) · Spike Milligan

Hemans's 'Casabianca' has given rise, as I mention above, to many imitations and parodies, all of which play with the opening image of the boy on the burning deck. Spike Milligan's is among the best known, in part because it so abruptly and so comically comes to a halt.

> The boy stood on the burning deck
> Whence all but he had fled –
> The twit!

In this poem, Walter de la Mare tells the story of a lone horseman's arrival at an empty house.

'Is there anybody there?' said the Traveller,
  Knocking on the moonlit door;
And his horse in the silence champed the grasses
  Of the forest's ferny floor:
And a bird flew up out of the turret,
  Above the Traveller's head:
And he smote upon the door again a second time;
  'Is there anybody there?' he said.
But no one descended to the Traveller;
  No head from the leaf-fringed sill
Leaned over and looked into his grey eyes,
  Where he stood perplexed and still.
But only a host of phantom listeners
  That dwelt in the lone house then
Stood listening in the quiet of the moonlight
  To that voice from the world of men:
Stood thronging the faint moonbeams on the dark stair,
  That goes down to the empty hall,
Hearkening in an air stirred and shaken
  By the lonely Traveller's call.
And he felt in his heart their strangeness,
  Their stillness answering his cry,
While his horse moved, cropping the dark turf,
  'Neath the starred and leafy sky;
For he suddenly smote on the door, even
  Louder, and lifted his head:—

203

'Tell them I came, and no one answered,
　　That I kept my word,' he said.
Never the least stir made the listeners,
　　Though every word he spake
Fell echoing through the shadowiness of the still house
　　From the one man left awake:
Ay, they heard his foot upon the stirrup,
　　And the sound of iron on stone,
And how the silence surged softly backward,
　　When the plunging hoofs were gone.

3 August · On the Grasshopper and Cricket · John Keats

Keats, in this sonnet about summer and winter, finds that there is poetry in the sounds of his environment. The grasshopper chirrups throughout summer, the cricket sings his song in the colds of winter, but all the year round the poet finds joy in the music of the natural world.

The poetry of earth is never dead:
    When all the birds are faint with the hot sun,
    And hide in cooling trees, a voice will run
From hedge to hedge about the new-mown mead;
That is the Grasshopper's – he takes the lead
    In summer luxury, – he has never done
    With his delights; for when tired out with fun
He rests at ease beneath some pleasant weed.
The poetry of earth is ceasing never:
    On a lone winter evening, when the frost
    Has wrought a silence, from the stove there shrills
The Cricket's song, in warmth increasing ever,
    And seems to one in drowsiness half lost,
    The Grasshopper's among some grassy hills.

3 August 1492 was the day on which the Italian explorer Christopher Columbus sailed westwards from Spain into the Atlantic Ocean, intending to find a new trade route to Asia. Instead, he arrived in America, and his expedition was one of the first European voyages to make contact with this 'New World'. This pithy little poem by the great writer and activist James Baldwin – a towering figure in the African-American Civil Rights movement in the 1920s – playfully subverts the idea that the colonial powers 'discovered' the American continent – where civilizations had prospered for millennia before Columbus arrived.

> Imagination
> creates the situation,
> and, then, the situation
> creates imagination.
>
> It may, of course,
> be the other way around:
> Columbus was discovered
> by what he found.

4 August · Minnie and Winnie · Alfred, Lord Tennyson

Tennyson wrote tightly metrical verse, but he was still a great experimenter in different kinds of metre. Both the lines 'Pink was the shell within' and 'Two bright stars' have three stressed, or heavy, syllables (*Pink*, *shell*, *-in*; *two*, *bright*, *stars*), but the first line has double the total syllables of the second. This is testament to how skilled Tennyson was at hearing the sounds of words, and it lends a playful tone to this poem about two ladies asleep in a seashell.

Minnie and Winnie
  Slept in a shell.
Sleep, little ladies!
  And they slept well.

Pink was the shell within,
  Silver without;
Sounds of the great sea
  Wander'd about.

Sleep, little ladies!
  Wake not soon!
Echo on echo
  Dies to the moon.

Two bright stars
  Peep'd into the shell.
'What are you dreaming of?
  Who can tell?'

Started a green linnet
Out of the croft;
Wake, little ladies,
The sun is aloft!

☽ 4 August • Meg Merrilies • John Keats

Compared to 'Minnie and Winnie', this poem by Keats has a very regular rhythm of unstressed and stressed syllables. Down, up, down, up, down, up. It follows in a long tradition of poems that sketch a portrait of an individual life, often an unusual one, before surprising us at the end with the fact that the subject of the poem has passed away.

Old Meg she was a Gipsy,
    And liv'd upon the Moors:
Her bed it was the brown heath turf,
    And her house was out of doors.

Her apples were swart blackberries,
    Her currants pods o' broom;
Her wine was dew of the wild white rose,
    Her book a churchyard tomb.

Her Brothers were the craggy hills,
    Her Sisters larchen trees –
Alone with her great family
    She liv'd as she did please.

No breakfast had she many a morn,
    No dinner many a noon,
And 'stead of supper she would stare
    Full hard against the Moon.

209

But every morn of woodbine fresh
    She made her garlanding,
And every night the dark glen Yew
    She wove, and she would sing.

And with her fingers old and brown
    She plaited Mats o' Rushes,
And gave them to the Cottagers
    She met among the Bushes.

Old Meg was brave as Margaret Queen
    And tall as Amazon:
An old red blanket cloak she wore;
    A chip hat had she on.
God rest her aged bones somewhere –
    She died full long agone!

'If' is a famous inspirational poem, written from the perspective of a father who is offering advice to his son.

If you can keep your head when all about you
    Are losing theirs and blaming it on you;
If you can trust yourself when all men doubt you,
    But make allowance for their doubting too;
If you can wait and not be tired by waiting,
    Or being lied about, don't deal in lies,
Or being hated, don't give way to hating,
    And yet don't look too good, nor talk too wise:

If you can dream – and not make dreams your master;
    If you can think – and not make thoughts your aim;
If you can meet with Triumph and Disaster
    And treat those two impostors just the same;
If you can bear to hear the truth you've spoken
    Twisted by knaves to make a trap for fools,
Or watch the things you gave your life to, broken,
    And stoop and build 'em up with worn-out tools:

If you can make one heap of all your winnings
    And risk it on one turn of pitch-and-toss,
And lose, and start again at your beginnings
    And never breathe a word about your loss;
If you can force your heart and nerve and sinew
    To serve your turn long after they are gone,
And so hold on when there is nothing in you
    Except the Will which says to them: 'Hold on!'

211

If you can talk with crowds and keep your virtue,
    Or walk with Kings – nor lose the common touch,
If neither foes nor loving friends can hurt you,
    If all men count with you, but none too much;
If you can fill the unforgiving minute
    With sixty seconds' worth of distance run,
Yours is the Earth and everything that's in it,
    And – which is more – you'll be a Man, my son!

Just like Kipling's 'If', this poem by Langston Hughes takes as its theme that simple two-letter word that can cover all things wished for, possible or imagined. While Kipling's poem lists a whole string of virtues – things that 'if' you can do them make you a wonderful person – Hughes's poem is all about the 'if' of having money.

If I had some small change
I'd buy me a mule,
Get on that mule and
Ride like a fool.

If I had some greenbacks
I'd buy me a Packard,
Fill it up with gas and
Drive that baby backward.

If I had a million
I'd get me a plane
And everybody in America'd
Think I was insane.

But I ain't got a million,

Fact is, ain't got a dime —

So just by if-ing

I have a good time!

6 August · The Horses · Edwin Muir

At 8.15 a.m. on 6 August 1945, the US Air Force
dropped an atomic bomb on the Japanese city of
Hiroshima. A few days later, a second bomb was
dropped on the city of Nagasaki. The Japanese
surrendered shortly after. The total death toll has been
estimated to be 126,000, and the two bombings remain
the only instances of the use of a nuclear weapon in
warfare. This poem by Edwin Muir imagines a nuclear
war that silences human society, yet nature returns to
the damaged world in the form of the horses.

Barely a twelvemonth after
The seven days war that put the world to sleep,
Late in the evening the strange horses came.
By then we had made our covenant with silence,
But in the first few days it was so still
We listened to our breathing and were afraid.
On the second day
The radios failed; we turned the knobs; no answer.
On the third day a warship passed us, heading north,
Dead bodies piled on the deck. On the sixth day
A plane plunged over us into the sea. Thereafter
Nothing. The radios dumb;
And still they stand in corners of our kitchens,
And stand, perhaps, turned on, in a million rooms
All over the world. But now if they should speak,
If on a sudden they should speak again,
If on the stroke of noon a voice should speak,
We would not listen, we would not let it bring
That old bad world that swallowed its children quick
At one great gulp. We would not have it again.

Sometimes we think of the nations lying asleep,
Curled blindly in impenetrable sorrow,
And then the thought confounds us with its strangeness.
The tractors lie about our fields; at evening
They look like dank sea-monsters couched and waiting.
We leave them where they are and let them rust:
'They'll moulder away and be like other loam.'
We make our oxen drag our rusty ploughs,
Long laid aside. We have gone back
Far past our fathers' land.
                    And then, that evening
Late in the summer the strange horses came.
We heard a distant tapping on the road,
A deepening drumming; it stopped, went on again
And at the corner changed to hollow thunder.
We saw the heads
Like a wild wave charging and were afraid.
We had sold our horses in our fathers' time
To buy new tractors. Now they were strange to us
As fabulous steeds set on an ancient shield.
Or illustrations in a book of knights.
We did not dare go near them. Yet they waited,
Stubborn and shy, as if they had been sent
By an old command to find our whereabouts
And that long-lost archaic companionship.
In the first moment we had never a thought
That they were creatures to be owned and used.
Among them were some half-a-dozen colts
Dropped in some wilderness of the broken world,
Yet new as if they had come from their own Eden.
Since then they have pulled our ploughs and borne our
    loads,
But that free servitude still can pierce our hearts.
Our life is changed; their coming our beginning.

How comforting do you find the idea of one true smile that can end all misery if it can be smiled only once in a lifetime?

There is a Smile of Love,
And there is a Smile of Deceit,
And there is a Smile of Smiles
In which these two Smiles meet,

And there is a Frown of Hate,
And there is a Frown of disdain,
And there is a Frown of Frowns
Which you strive to forget in vain,

For it sticks in the Hearts deep Core
And it sticks in the deep Back bone,
And no Smile that ever was smil'd,
But only one Smile alone,

That betwixt the Cradle & Grave
It only once Smil'd can be;
But, when it once is Smil'd,
There's an end to all Misery.

7 August · The Meadow Mouse · Theodore Roethke

The great nature poet Wordsworth wrote how 'love of nature' led him to 'love of Mankind'. In this spirit, Roethke's experience looking after a helpless field mouse leads the poet to reflect on all innocent things and beings. Against his will, he builds a strong devotion to a creature as humble as the mouse.

I

In a shoe box stuffed in an old nylon stocking
Sleeps the baby mouse I found in the meadow,
Where he trembled and shook beneath a stick
Till I caught him up by the tail and brought him in,
Cradled in my hand,
A little quaker, the whole body of him trembling,
His absurd whiskers sticking out like a cartoon-mouse,
His feet like small leaves,
Little lizard-feet,
Whitish and spread wide when he tried to struggle away,
Wriggling like a minuscule puppy.

Now he's eaten his three kinds of cheese and drunk
    from his bottle-cap watering-trough –
So much he just lies in one corner,
His tail curled under him, his belly big
As his head; his bat-like ears
Twitching, tilting toward the least sound.

217

Do I imagine he no longer trembles
When I come close to him?
He seems no longer to tremble.

II

But this morning the shoe-box house on the back porch
    is empty.
Where has he gone, my meadow mouse,
My thumb of a child that nuzzled in my palm? –
To run under the hawk's wing,
Under the eye of the great owl watching from the elm-tree,
To live by courtesy of the shrike, the snake, the tom-cat.

I think of the nestling fallen into the deep grass,
The turtle gasping in the dusty rubble of the highway,
The paralytic stunned in the tub, and the water rising, –
All things innocent, hapless, forsaken.

🌙 7 August • A Poison Tree • William Blake

This poem uses a central image of a tree that echoes the Tree of Knowledge in the Biblical story. Blake seems to be suggesting that if you don't express your anger immediately, then it will grow and make you bitter.

I was angry with my friend:
I told my wrath, my wrath did end.
I was angry with my foe:
I told it not, my wrath did grow.

And I water'd it in fears,
Night & morning with my tears;
And I sunned it with smiles,
And with soft deceitful wiles.

And it grew both day and night.
Till it bore an apple bright;
And my foe beheld it shine,
And he knew that it was mine,

And into my garden stole
When the night had veil'd the pole:
In the morning glad I see
My foe outstretch'd beneath the tree.

8 August · *from* A Song About Myself · John Keats

The schoolboy in Keats's poem expects to find everything completely different in another country, but instead he finds it pretty much exactly the same. It might not be the most lyrical or complicated poetry penned by Keats, but it is imbued with a clear and timeless wisdom about the commonalities that bind people from all corners of the world – or in this slightly less global case, England and Scotland. It is a lesson that should still be heeded today by everyone, from naughty schoolboys to adults who ought to know better.

There was a naughty boy,
  And a naughty boy was he,
He ran away to Scotland
  The people for to see –
      Then he found
      That the ground
      Was as hard,
      That a yard
      Was as long,
      That a song
      Was as merry,
      That a cherry
      Was as red,
      That lead
      Was as weighty,
      That fourscore
      Was as eighty,

That a door
Was as wooden
As in England –
So he stood in his shoes
And he wondered,
He wondered,
He stood in his
Shoes and he wondered.

This poem refers to the death of Sir Francis Drake, who is said to have commanded on his deathbed that his ship's drum be taken back to his home in Devon. If it is beaten at times of national crisis, so the story goes, he will rise again to save England. 8 August 1588 is the date the English navy defeated the Spanish Armada.

Drake he's in his hammock an' a thousand miles away,
    (Capten, art tha sleepin' there below?)
Slung atween the round shot in Nombre Dios Bay,
    An' dreamin' arl the time o' Plymouth Hoe.
Yarnder lumes the Island, yarnder lie the ships,
    Wi' sailor lads a-dancing' heel-an'-toe,
An' the shore-lights flashin', an' the night-tide dashin',
    He sees et arl so plainly as he saw et long ago.

Drake he was a Devon man, an' ruled the Devon seas,
    (Capten, art tha' sleepin' there below?)
Rovin' tho' his death fell, he went wi' heart at ease,
    A' dreamin' arl the time o' Plymouth Hoe.
'Take my drum to England, hang et by the shore,
    Strike et when your powder's runnin' low;
If the Dons sight Devon, I'll quit the port o' Heaven,
    An' drum them up the Channel as we drumm'd them
      long ago.'

Drake he's in his hammock till the great Armadas come,
    (Capten, art tha sleepin' there below?)
Slung atween the round shot, listenin' for the drum,
    An' dreamin arl the time o' Plymouth Hoe.
Call him on the deep sea, call him up the Sound,
    Call him when ye sail to meet the foe;
Where the old trade's plyin' an' the old flag flyin'
    They shall find him ware an' wakin', as they found
        him long ago!

Britain has a long history of being a seafaring nation.
This poem describes cargoes from all over the world.

Quinquireme of Nineveh from distant Ophir,
Rowing home to haven in sunny Palestine,
With a cargo of ivory,
And apes and peacocks,
Sandalwood, cedarwood, and sweet white wine.

Stately Spanish galleon coming from the Isthmus,
Dipping through the Tropics by the palm-green shores,
With a cargo of diamonds,
Emeralds, amythysts,
Topazes, and cinnamon, and gold moidores.

Dirty British coaster with a salt-caked smoke stack,
Butting through the Channel in the mad March days,
With a cargo of Tyne coal,
Road-rails, pig-lead,
Firewood, iron-ware, and cheap tin trays.

☾ 9 August · The Fairy School under the Loch · John Rice

Poetry can make everyday experiences seem fantastic, and it can make the fantastic seem everyday. In this beautiful imagining of a school for fairies, hidden away beneath the surface of a loch, classes go on as normal despite being held deep underwater.

The wind sings its gusty song.
The bell rings its rusty ring.
The underwater fairy children
dive and swim through school gates.
They do not get wet.

The waves flick their flashing spray.
A school of fish wriggles its scaly way.
The underwater fairy children
learn their liquidy lessons.
Their reading books are always dry.

The seals straighten in a stretchy mass.
Teresa the Teacher flits and floats from class to class.
The underwater fairy children
count, play, sing and recite,
their clothes not in the least bit damp.

The rocks creak in their cracking skin.
A fairy boat drifts into a loch of time.
The underwater fairy children
lived, learned and left this life –
their salty stories now dry as their cracked wings.

225

10 August · I'd Love to Be a Fairy's Child · Robert Graves

Robert Graves was a prolific novelist and poet, most famous for the fictional autobiography of the Roman Emperor Claudius, *I, Claudius*. In this poem, the speaker jealously imagines how wonderful it would be to have fairies for parents – that way he'd have more pocket money than he could ever dream of!

Children born of fairy stock
Never need for shirt or frock,
Never want for food or fire,
Always get their heart's desire:
Jingle pockets full of gold,
Marry when they're seven years old,
Every fairy child may keep
Two strong ponies and ten sheep;
All have houses, each his own,
Built of brick or granite stone;
They live on cherries, they run wild –
I'd love to be a fairy's child.

A gymkhana is an equestrian event that consists of trials and timed games played while riding horses and ponies. And that's what John Betjeman is making fun of in this poem.

It's awf'lly bad luck on Diana,
  Her ponies have swallowed their bits;
She fished down their throats with a spanner
  And frightened them all into fits.

So now she's attempting to borrow.
  Do lend her some bits, Mummy, *do*;
I'll lend her my own for to-morrow,
  But to-day *I*'ll be wanting them too.

Just look at Prunella on Guzzle,
  The wizardest pony on earth;
Why doesn't she slacken his muzzle
  And tighten the breech in his girth?

I say, Mummy, there's Mrs. Geyser
  And doesn't she look pretty sick?
I bet it's because Mona Lisa
  Was hit on the hock with a brick.

Miss Blewitt says Monica threw it,
  But Monica says it was Joan,
And Joan's very thick with Miss Blewitt,
  So Monica's sulking alone.

And Margaret failed in her paces,
    Her withers got tied in a noose,
So her coronets caught in the traces
    And now all her fetlocks are loose.

Oh, it's me now. I'm terribly nervous.
    I wonder if Smudges will shy.
She's practically certain to swerve as
    Her Pelham is over one eye.

*

Oh wasn't it naughty of Smudges?
    Oh, Mummy, I'm sick with disgust.
She threw me in front of the Judges,
    And my silly old collarbone's bust.

11 August · Verses written to the Queen of England · Mary, Queen of Scots

On 11 August 1586, Mary, Queen of Scots, was arrested for her involvement in the Babington Plot – a plot to assassinate Mary's cousin, Elizabeth I. Mary was beheaded under Elizabeth's orders the following year. These lines, attributed to Mary and supposedly sent to Elizabeth, express Mary's anxiety about the likelihood of her own execution.

A single thought which benefits and harms me
Bitter and sweet alternate endlessly in my heart.
Between hope and fear this thought weighs down on me
So much that peace and rest flee from me

So, dear sister, if this paper reiterates
My pressing desire to see you;
It is because I see in pain and sorrow
The immediate outcome if this request should fail.

I have seen the ship blown by contrary winds
On the high seas, near to the harbour mouth
And the calm turning to troubled water

Likewise (sister) I live in fear and terror
Not on account of you, but because there are times
When Fortune can destroy sail and rigging at once.

11 August · Triolet · G. K. Chesterton

A triolet is a type of poetic form which originated in French medieval poetry. For the most part it is a poem of eight lines, in which the first, fourth and seventh lines are identical. This poem is a joyful example of how a simple idea can create a comic picture, in this case that of a jellyfish falling down the stairs.

> I wish I were a jellyfish
> That cannot fall downstairs;
> Of all the things I wish to wish
> I wish I were a jellyfish
> That hasn't any cares
> And doesn't even have to wish
> 'I wish I were a jellyfish
> That cannot fall downstairs.'

12 August · Manly Sports · Marion Bernstein

12 August is known as the 'Glorious Twelfth', and it marks the start of the shooting season for grouse. Here, the radical feminist poet Marion Bernstein ridicules and underlines the cruelty of hunting by presenting it, mockingly, as a daring and manly sport. Hovering beneath Bernstein's ironic praise is her disdain for the misplaced sense of pride and courage felt by men who view themselves 'brave knights' when they slaughter defenceless animals.

How brave is the hunter who nobly will dare
On horseback to follow the small timid hare;
Oh! ye soldiers who fall in defence of your flag,
What are you to the hero who brings down the stag?

Bright eyes glance admiring, soft hearts give their loves
To the knight who shoots best in 'the tourney of doves';
Nothing else with such slaughtering feats can compare,
To win manly applause, or the smiles of the fair.

A cheer for fox-hunting! Come all who can dare
Track this dangerous animal down to its lair;
'Tis first trapped, then set free for the huntsmen to
    follow
With horses and hounds, and with heartstirring halloo!

The brave knights on the moor when the grouse are
    a-drive,
Slay so many, you'd think, there'd be none left alive;
Oh! the desperate daring of slaughtering grouse,
Can only be matched in a real slaughterhouse.

The angler finds true Anglo-Saxon delight,
In trapping small fish, who so foolishly bite,
He enjoys the wild terror of creatures so weak,
And what manlier pleasures can any one seek?

12 August • Blackberry-Picking • Seamus Heaney

August in England is blackberry season – as summer slowly turns into autumn, the hedgerows become covered in berries. This poem by Seamus Heaney brilliantly evokes the rich sights and smells of late summer, and the deliciousness of freshly picked blackberries: 'sweet / Like thickened wine'.

For Philip Hobsbaum

Late August, given heavy rain and sun
For a full week, the blackberries would ripen.
At first, just one, a glossy purple clot
Among others, red, green, hard as a knot.
You ate that first one and its flesh was sweet
Like thickened wine: summer's blood was in it
Leaving stains upon the tongue and lust for
Picking. Then red ones inked up and that hunger
Sent us out with milk cans, pea tins, jam pots
Where briars scratched and wet grass bleached our boots.
Round hayfields, cornfields and potato drills
We trekked and picked until the cans were full,
Until the tinkling bottom had been covered
With green ones, and on top big dark blobs burned
Like a plate of eyes. Our hands were peppered
With thorn pricks, our palms sticky as Bluebeard's.

233

We hoarded the fresh berries in the byre.
But when the bath was filled we found a fur,
A rat-grey fungus, glutting on our cache.
The juice was stinking too. Once off the bush
The fruit fermented, the sweet flesh would turn sour.
I always felt like crying. It wasn't fair
That all the lovely canfuls smelt of rot.
Each year I hoped they'd keep, knew they would not.

13 August · Shakespeare at School · Wendy Cope

In this witty sonnet, Wendy Cope imagines the master
of the form, Shakespeare, in his schoolboy days,
regaling an audience of bored classmates.

Forty boys on benches with their quills,
Six days a week through almost all the year,
Long hours of Latin with relentless drills
And repetition, all enforced by fear.
I picture Shakespeare sitting near the back,
Indulging in a risky bit of fun
By exercising his prodigious knack
Of thinking up an idiotic pun,
And whispering his gem to other boys,
Some of whom could not suppress their mirth –
Behaviour that unfailingly annoys
Any teacher anywhere on earth.
The fun was over when the master spoke:
Will Shakespeare, come up here and share the joke.

235

The Battle of Blenheim, one of the major battles of the
War of the Spanish Succession, was fought on 13 August
1704.

It was a summer evening,
  Old Kaspar's work was done,
And he before his cottage door
  Was sitting in the sun;
And by him sported on the green
His little grandchild Wilhelmine.

She saw her brother Peterkin
  Roll something large and round,
Which he beside the rivulet
  In playing there had found;
He came to ask what he had found,
That was so large, and smooth, and round.

Old Kaspar took it from the boy,
  Who stood expectant by;
And then the old man shook his head,
  And, with a natural sigh,
''Tis some poor fellow's skull,' said he,
'Who fell in the great victory.

'I find them in the garden,
  For there's many here about;
And often when I go to plough
  The ploughshare turns them out.
For many thousand men,' said he,
'Were slain in that great victory.'

'Now tell us what 'twas all about,'
    Young Peterkin, he cries;
And little Wilhelmine looks up
    With wonder-waiting eyes;
'Now tell us all about the war,
And what they fought each other for.'

'It was the English,' Kaspar cried,
    'Who put the French to rout;
But what they fought each other for,
    I could not well make out;
But everybody said,' quoth he,
'That 'twas a famous victory.

'My father lived at Blenheim then,
    Yon little stream hard by;
They burnt his dwelling to the ground,
    And he was forced to fly;
So with his wife and child he fled,
Nor had he where to rest his head.

'With fire and sword the country round
    Was wasted far and wide,
And many a childing mother then
    And newborn baby died;
But things like that, you know, must be
At every famous victory.

'They say it was a shocking sight
    After the field was won;
For many thousand bodies here
    Lay rotting in the sun:
But things like that, you know, must be
After a famous victory.

237

'Great praise the Duke of Marlbro' won,
    And our good Prince Eugene.'
'Why, 'twas a very wicked thing!'
    Said little Wilhelmine.
'Nay . . . nay . . . my little girl,' quoth he,
'It was a famous victory.

'And everybody praised the Duke
    Who this great fight did win.'
'But what good came of it at last?'
    Quoth little Peterkin.
'Why that I cannot tell,' said he,
'But 'twas a famous victory.'

14 August · *from* Macbeth · William Shakespeare

On or around 14 August 1040, King Duncan I of Scotland was murdered by his cousin Macbeth – the historical source for Shakespeare's great play. At this point in the play, Macbeth has killed Duncan, and is now focused on his next target, Banquo. Macbeth fears that according to the witches' prophecy, it is Banquo's heirs ('issue'), not Macbeth's own, who will become kings hereafter.

> To be thus is nothing,
> But to be safely thus. Our fears in Banquo
> Stick deep, and in his royalty of nature
> Reigns that which would be feared. 'Tis much he dares,
> And to that dauntless temper of his mind
> He hath a wisdom that doth guide his valour
> To act in safety. There is none but he
> Whose being I do fear; and under him
> My genius is rebuked, as it is said
> Mark Antony's was by Caesar. He chid the sisters
> When first they put the name of king upon me,
> And bade them speak to him. Then, prophet-like,
> They hailed him father to a line of kings.
> Upon my head they placed a fruitless crown
> And put a barren sceptre in my grip,
> Thence to be wrenched with an unlineal hand,
> No son of mine succeeding. If 't be so,
> For Banquo's issue have I filed my mind,
> For them the gracious Duncan have I murdered;

239

Put rancours in the vessel of my peace
Only for them, and mine eternal jewel
Given to the common enemy of man,
To make them kings, the seed of Banquo kings!
Rather than so, come Fate into the list,
And champion me to th' utterance.

In this poem, Anthony Watts paints a vivid picture of the twilight scene he is describing using only a few words in each line.

> The old world turns
>   in its rusty socket;
> a ragged sky burns;
> the sea slops
>   in the moon's bucket;
> the sun's penny drops.

15 August · A Flea and a Fly · Ogden Nash

When two words are pronounced the same but are spelt differently, they are called homophones – meaning 'same sound'. This poem makes use of the same and similar sounds to create an amusing effect in a conversation between a flea and a fly.

A flea and a fly in a flue
Were imprisoned, so what could they do?
Said the fly, 'Let us flee!'
'Let us fly!' said the flea
So they flew through a flaw in the flue.

15 August · *from* Macbeth · William Shakespeare

This speech is a soliloquy, delivered by Macbeth straight after he has received news of his wife's death. The historical Scottish King Macbeth was killed on this day in 1057 by the future King Malcolm III, though Shakespeare's play is far from being a reliable 'history' of his reign.

Tomorrow, and tomorrow, and tomorrow,
Creeps in this petty pace from day to day,
To the last syllable of recorded time;
And all our yesterdays have lighted fools
The way to dusty death. Out, out, brief candle!
Life's but a walking shadow, a poor player,
That struts and frets his hour upon the stage,
And then is heard no more. It is a tale
Told by an idiot, full of sound and fury,
Signifying nothing.

16 August · Musée des Beaux Arts · W. H. Auden

This poem by the Anglo-American poet Auden is an example of 'ekphrasis' – a Greek term for when a visual work of art, like a painting, is described in a textual work of art, like a poem. If it's true that a picture can paint a thousand words, then how should words go about painting a picture? The painting is *Landscape with the Fall of Icarus* by Pieter Brueghel the Elder, which Auden saw in Brussels. It depicts the myth of Icarus, in which an over-ambitious boy flies with wings held together with wax too close to the sun; the wings melt, and he plummets to his death. Yet in spite of the extraordinary sight of a boy falling from the sky, the other figures in the painting continue with life as normal, calmly ignoring the tragic event.

About suffering they were never wrong,
The Old Masters: how well they understood
Its human position; how it takes place
While someone else is eating or opening a window or just
    walking dully along;
How, when the aged are reverently, passionately waiting
For the miraculous birth, there always must be
Children who did not specially want it to happen, skating
On a pond at the edge of the wood:
They never forgot
That even the dreadful martyrdom must run its course
Anyhow in a corner, some untidy spot

Where the dogs go on with their doggy life and the
     torturer's horse
Scratches its innocent behind on a tree.

In Brueghel's *Icarus*, for instance: how everything turns
     away
Quite leisurely from the disaster; the ploughman may
Have heard the splash, the forsaken cry,
But for him it was not an important failure; the sun shone
As it had to on the white legs disappearing into the green
Water; and the expensive delicate ship that must have
     seen
Something amazing, a boy falling out of the sky,
had somewhere to get to and sailed calmly on.

☪ 16 August · The Viking Terror · Anon., translated by Kuno Meyer

Originally written in Old Irish, this poem was found in the margin of a manuscript which has been dated to around 850 AD – a time in which Irish coastal communities lived in constant fear of vicious Viking raiding parties. While we might think of bad weather as irritating, for the anonymous Irish poet who wrote these lines, turbulent seas were a blessing, guaranteeing safety from the Viking longboats which could not be sailed safely in a storm.

Bitter is the wind tonight.
It tosses the ocean's white hair:
Tonight I fear not the fierce warriors of Norway
Coursing on the Irish Sea.

Like the poem that is included above as the entry for
28 June, this poem is taken from the great American
writer John Updike's collection of children's poetry,
A Child's Calendar.

The sprinkler twirls.
The summer wanes.
The pavement wears
Popsicle stains.

The playground grass
Is worn to dust.
The weary swings
Creak, creak with rust.

The trees are bored
With being green.
Some people leave
The local scene

And go to seaside
Bungalows
And take off nearly
All their clothes.

Like W. H. Auden's above, this poem by Robert Browning is another example of ekphrasis. It's thought to be about a portrait of 'Lucrezia de' Medici'. The poem is a dramatic monologue, spoken by a 'Ferrara' – the 5th Duke of Ferrara, who married Lucrezia in 1558. Only a few years into their married life, the Duke abandoned his young wife; she died shortly afterwards. While most historians claim that Lucrezia died of tuberculosis, some believe that she was poisoned – possibly by her own husband.

That's my last Duchess painted on the wall,
Looking as if she were alive. I call
That piece a wonder, now; Frà Pandolf's hands
Worked busily a day, and there she stands.
Will't please you sit and look at her? I said
'Frà Pandolf' by design, for never read
Strangers like you that pictured countenance,
The depth and passion of its earnest glance,
But to myself they turned (since none puts by
The curtain I have drawn for you, but I)
And seemed as they would ask me, if they durst,
How such a glance came there; so, not the first
Are you to turn and ask thus. Sir, 'twas not
Her husband's presence only, called that spot
Of joy into the Duchess' cheek: perhaps
Frà Pandolf chanced to say, 'Her mantle laps
Over my lady's wrist too much,' or 'Paint

Must never hope to reproduce the faint
Half-flush that dies along her throat.' Such stuff
Was courtesy, she thought, and cause enough
For calling up that spot of joy. She had
A heart – how shall I say? – too soon made glad,
Too easily impressed; she liked whate'er
She looked on, and her looks went everywhere.
Sir, 'twas all one! My favour at her breast,
The dropping of the daylight in the West,
The bough of cherries some officious fool
Broke in the orchard for her, the white mule
She rode with round the terrace – all and each
Would draw from her alike the approving speech,
Or blush, at least. She thanked men – good! but
   thanked
Somehow – I know not how – as if she ranked
My gift of a nine-hundred-years-old name
With anybody's gift. Who'd stoop to blame
This sort of trifling? Even had you skill
In speech – which I have not – to make your will
Quite clear to such an one, and say, 'Just this
Or that in you disgusts me; here you miss,
Or there exceed the mark' – and if she let
Herself be lessoned so, nor plainly set
Her wits to yours, forsooth, and made excuse –
E'en then would be some stooping; and I choose
Never to stoop. Oh, sir, she smiled, no doubt,
Whene'er I passed her; but who passed without
Much the same smile? This grew; I gave commands;
Then all smiles stopped together. There she stands
As if alive. Will't please you rise? We'll meet
The company below, then. I repeat,
The Count your master's known munificence
Is ample warrant that no just pretence

Of mine for dowry will be disallowed;
Though his fair daughter's self, as I avowed
At starting, is my object. Nay, we'll go
Together down, sir. Notice Neptune, though,
Taming a sea-horse, thought a rarity,
Which Claus of Innsbruck cast in bronze for me!

🌑 **18 August** · Don't Let That Horse · Lawrence Ferlinghetti

This is another ekphrastic poem. This time, though, ekphrasis is used to comic effect: Marc Chagall's *Equestrienne* – a very strange painting in which a couple ride a horse who is munching, bizarrely, on a violin – is transformed into a story about the painter himself. The poem builds to a magnificent pun.

Don't let that horse
                    eat that violin

    cried Chagall's mother

                    But he
            kept right on
                    painting

And became famous

And kept on painting
                    The Horse With Violin In Mouth
And when he finally finished it
he jumped up upon the horse
                    and rode away
        waving the violin

And then with a low bow gave it
to the first naked nude he ran across

And there were no strings
                    attached

Matthew Arnold must surely have had Tennyson's 1830
effort, 'The Merman' (see 23 July), in mind when he
wrote his own narrative poem in 1849 about a creature
human from the waist up, fish from the waist down.
Where Tennyson's lustful, obnoxious merman spent his
time chasing mermaids, Arnold's titular character is left
lonely and forlorn after his human wife leaves him.

Come, dear children, let us away;
Down and away below!
Now my brothers call from the bay,
Now the great winds shoreward blow,
Now the salt tides seaward flow;
Now the wild white horses play,
Champ and chafe and toss in the spray.
Children dear, let us away!
This way, this way!

Call her once before you go—
Call once yet!
In a voice that she will know:
'Margaret! Margaret!'
Children's voices should be dear
(Call once more) to a mother's ear;

Children's voices, wild with pain—
Surely she will come again!
Call her once and come away;

This way, this way!
'Mother dear, we cannot stay!
The wild white horses foam and fret.'
Margaret! Margaret!

Come, dear children, come away down;
Call no more!
One last look at the white-wall'd town
And the little grey church on the windy shore,
Then come down!
She will not come though you call all day;
Come away, come away!

Children dear, was it yesterday
We heard the sweet bells over the bay?
In the caverns where we lay,
Through the surf and through the swell,
The far-off sound of a silver bell?
Sand-strewn caverns, cool and deep,
Where the winds are all asleep;
Where the spent lights quiver and gleam,
Where the salt weed sways in the stream,
Where the sea-beasts, ranged all round,
Feed in the ooze of their pasture-ground;
Where the sea-snakes coil and twine,
Dry their mail and bask in the brine;
Where great whales come sailing by,
Sail and sail, with unshut eye,
Round the world for ever and aye?
When did music come this way?
Children dear, was it yesterday?

Children dear, was it yesterday
(Call yet once) that she went away?

Once she sate with you and me,
On a red gold throne in the heart of the sea,
And the youngest sate on her knee.
She comb'd its bright hair, and she tended it well,
When down swung the sound of a far-off bell.
She sigh'd, she look'd up through the clear green sea;
She said: 'I must go, to my kinsfolk pray
In the little grey church on the shore to-day.
'Twill be Easter-time in the world—ah me!
And I lose my poor soul, Merman! here with thee.'
I said: 'Go up, dear heart, through the waves;
Say thy prayer, and come back to the kind sea-caves!'
She smiled, she went up through the surf in the bay.
Children dear, was it yesterday?

Children dear, were we long alone?
'The sea grows stormy, the little ones moan;
Long prayers,' I said, 'in the world they say;
Come!' I said; and we rose through the surf in the bay.
We went up the beach, by the sandy down
Where the sea-stocks bloom, to the white-wall'd town;
Through the narrow paved streets, where all was still,
To the little grey church on the windy hill.
From the church came a murmur of folk at their prayers,
But we stood without in the cold blowing airs.
We climb'd on the graves, on the stones worn with rains,
And we gazed up the aisle through the small leaded panes.
She sate by the pillar; we saw her clear:
'Margaret, hist! come quick, we are here!
Dear heart,' I said, 'we are long alone;
The sea grows stormy, the little ones moan.'
But, ah, she gave me never a look,
For her eyes were seal'd to the holy book!
Loud prays the priest; shut stands the door.

Come away, children, call no more!
Come away, come down, call no more!

Down, down, down!
Down to the depths of the sea!
She sits at her wheel in the humming town,
Singing most joyfully.
Hark what she sings: 'O joy, O joy,
For the humming street, and the child with its toy!
For the priest, and the bell, and the holy well;
For the wheel where I spun,
And the blessed light of the sun!'
And so she sings her fill,
Singing most joyfully,
Till the spindle drops from her hand,
And the whizzing wheel stands still.
She steals to the window, and looks at the sand,
And over the sand at the sea;
And her eyes are set in a stare;
And anon there breaks a sigh,
And anon there drops a tear,
From a sorrow-clouded eye,
And a heart sorrow-laden,
A long, long sigh;
For the cold strange eyes of a little Mermaiden
And the gleam of her golden hair.

Come away, away children
Come children, come down!
The hoarse wind blows coldly;
Lights shine in the town.
She will start from her slumber
When gusts shake the door;
She will hear the winds howling,

255

Will hear the waves roar.
We shall see, while above us
The waves roar and whirl,
A ceiling of amber,
A pavement of pearl.
Singing: 'Here came a mortal,
But faithless was she!
And alone dwell for ever
The kings of the sea.'

But, children, at midnight,
When soft the winds blow,
When clear falls the moonlight,
When spring-tides are low;
When sweet airs come seaward
From heaths starr'd with broom,
And high rocks throw mildly
On the blanch'd sands a gloom;
Up the still, glistening beaches,
Up the creeks we will hie,
Over banks of bright seaweed
The ebb-tide leaves dry.
We will gaze, from the sand-hills,
At the white, sleeping town;
At the church on the hill-side—
And then come back down.
Singing: 'There dwells a loved one,
But cruel is she!
She left lonely for ever
The kings of the sea.'

256

In this poem, Stevie Smith's narrator tells a strange,
magical story about a princess who marries a fairy king,
and moves to a fairy kingdom near a 'forlorn sea'.

Our Princess married
A fairy King,
It was a sensational
Wedding.

Now they live in a palace
Of porphyry,
Far, far away,
By the forlorn sea.

Sometimes people visit them,
Last week they invited me;
That is how I can tell you
They live by a forlorn sea.

(They said: Here's a magic carpet,
Come on this,
And when you arrive
We will give you a big kiss.)

I play in the palace garden,
I climb the sycamore tree,
Sometimes I swim
In the forlorn sea.

The King and the Princess are shadowy,
Yet beautiful,
They are waited on by white cats,
Who are dutiful.

It is like a dream
When they kiss and cuddle me,
But I like it, I like it,
I do not wish to break free.

So I eat all they give me
Because I have read
If you eat fairy food
You will never wake up in your own bed,

But will go on living,
As has happened to me,
Far, far away
By a forlorn sea.

☾ **19 August** • And Death Shall Have No Dominion • Dylan Thomas

Dylan Thomas wrote this poem in 1933, after the horrors of the First World War and during the political tensions that were mounting towards the Second. The title is taken from the book of Romans in the New Testament.

And death shall have no dominion.
Dead man naked they shall be one
With the man in the wind and the west moon;
When their bones are picked clean and the clean bones
    gone,
They shall have stars at elbow and foot;
Though they go mad they shall be sane,
Though they sink through the sea they shall rise again;
Though lovers be lost love shall not;
And death shall have no dominion.

And death shall have no dominion.
Under the windings of the sea
They lying long shall not die windily;
Twisting on racks when sinews give way,
Strapped to a wheel, yet they shall not break;
Faith in their hands shall snap in two,
And the unicorn evils run them through;
Split all ends up they shan't crack;
And death shall have no dominion.

And death shall have no dominion.
No more may gulls cry at their ears
Or waves break loud on the seashores;
Where blew a flower may a flower no more
Lift its head to the blows of the rain;
Though they be mad and dead as nails,
Heads of the characters hammer through daisies;
Break in the sun till the sun breaks down,
And death shall have no dominion.

☀ **20 August** · How Many Seconds in a Minute? · Christina Rossetti

This poem by Christina Rossetti is about the things we can add up, and the things we cannot. Her couplets guide us through larger and larger spans of time, before she reaches the limit: how big is time itself? For that question, she jokes, there is no way of completing the rhyme.

How many seconds in a minute?
Sixty, and no more in it.

How many minutes in an hour?
Sixty for sun and shower.

How many hours in a day?
Twenty-four for work and play.

How many days in a week?
Seven both to hear and speak.

How many weeks in a month?
Four, as the swift moon runn'th.

How many months in a year?
Twelve the almanack makes clear.

How many years in an age?
One hundred says the sage.

How many ages in time?
No one knows the rhyme.

C 20 August · Thunder · Elizabeth Bishop

This poem uses a fantasy world of gods and giants to
explain the causes of thunder.

And suddenly the giants tired of play. –
With huge, rough hands they flung the gods' gold balls
And silver harps and mirrors at the walls
Of Heaven, and trod, ashamed, where lay
The loveliness of flowers. Frightened Day
On white feet ran from out the temple halls,
The blundering dark was filled with great war-calls,
And Beauty, shamed, slunk silently away.

Be quiet, little wind among the leaves
That turn pale faces to the coming storm.
Be quiet, little foxes in your lairs,
And birds and mice be still – a giant grieves
For his forgotten might. Hark now the warm
And heavy stumbling down the leaden stairs!

21 August · Say Not the Struggle Nought Availeth · Arthur Hugh Clough

Arthur Hugh Clough was a Victorian poet, but he was also the secretarial assistant to the founder of modern nursing Florence Nightingale, his wife's cousin. The message of this poem is one of hope. Through the metaphors of a battlefield, the ocean's waves, and the rising sun, Clough is saying: don't give up, keep fighting – better things are on the way.

Say not the struggle nought availeth,
  The labour and the wounds are vain,
The enemy faints not, nor faileth,
  And as things have been they remain.

If hopes were dupes, fears may be liars;
  It may be, in yon smoke concealed,
Your comrades chase e'en now the fliers,
  And, but for you, possess the field.

For while the tired waves, vainly breaking,
  Seem here no painful inch to gain,
Far back through creeks and inlets making
  Comes silent, flooding in, the main,

And not by eastern windows only,
  When daylight comes, comes in the light,
In front the sun climbs slow, how slowly,
  But westward, look, the land is bright.

☾ 21 August · Bed in Summer ·
Robert Louis Stevenson

Robert Louis Stevenson spent much of his childhood bed-bound due to illness, so he may well have had a particularly sharp memory of the misery of staying in bed while the world outside enjoys the longer hours of light in the summertime.

In winter I get up at night
And dress by yellow candle-light.
In summer, quite the other way,
I have to go to bed by day.

I have to go to bed and see
The birds still hopping on the tree,
Or hear the grown-up people's feet
Still going past me in the street.

And does it not seem hard to you,
When all the sky is clear and blue,
And I should like so much to play,
To have to go to bed by day?

264

22 August · Who Would True Valour See · John Bunyan

On this day in 1642, the English Civil War broke out. Battles were fought between the Parliamentarians and Royalists until 1651. John Bunyan, a Puritan preacher and writer, spent three years fighting for the Parliamentarian army. He is best remembered for the religious allegory *The Pilgrim's Progress*.

Who would true Valour see
Let him come hither;
One here will Constant be,
Come Wind, come Weather.
There's no Discouragement,
Shall make him once Relent,
His first avow'd Intent,
To be a Pilgrim.

Who so beset him round,
With dismal Stories,
Do but themselves Confound;
His Strength the more is.
No Lyon can him fright,
He'l with a Gyant Fight,
But he will have a right,
To be a Pilgrim.

Hobgoblin, nor foul Fiend,
Can daunt his Spirit:
He knows, he at the end,

Shall Life Inherit.
Then Fancies fly away,
He'll fear not what men say,
He'll labour Night and Day,
To be a Pilgrim.

22 August · Humpty Dumpty · Anon.

On this day in 1485, Richard III was defeated by Henry Tudor at the Battle of Bosworth. There is a popular theory that Humpty Dumpty in this English nursery rhyme symbolizes Richard III, and his 'great fall' represents Richard falling from his horse – an incident that has become part of the accepted history due to the immortal scene in Shakespeare's eponymous play, but remains disputed. One also can't help but wonder if there's something in the air on this date that provokes conflict, as 22 August also marked the start of the English Civil War some 150 years later.

> Humpty Dumpty sat on a wall,
> Humpty Dumpty had a great fall;
> All the king's horses and all the king's men
> Couldn't put Humpty together again.

· Little Red Riding Hood · Roald Dahl

In this poem from his collection *Revolting Rhymes*, Roald Dahl takes the familiar story of Little Red Riding Hood and gives the ending an exciting, gruesome twist. Rather than relying upon the woodsman to come and save her and her grandmother, Dahl's stylish, dangerous Little Red Riding Hood is perfectly capable of taking care of herself . . .

As soon as Wolf began to feel
That he would like a decent meal,
He went and knocked on Grandma's door.
When Grandma opened it, she saw
The sharp white teeth, the horrid grin,
And Wolfie said, 'May I come in?'
Poor Grandmamma was terrified,
'He's going to eat me up!' she cried.

And she was absolutely right.
He ate her up in one big bite.
But Grandmamma was small and tough,
And Wolfie wailed, 'That's not enough!
I haven't yet begun to feel
That I have had a decent meal!'
He ran around the kitchen yelping,
'I've got to have a second helping!'
Then added with a frightful leer,
'I'm therefore going to wait right here
Till Little Miss Red Riding Hood

Comes home from walking in the wood.'
He quickly put on Grandma's clothes
(Of course he hadn't eaten those).
He dressed himself in coat and hat.
He put on shoes, and after that,
He even brushed and curled his hair,
Then sat himself in Grandma's chair.
In came the little girl in red.
She stopped. She stared. And then she said,

'What great big ears you have, Grandma.'
'All the better to hear you with,'
the Wolf replied.
'What great big eyes you have, Grandma.'
said Little Red Riding Hood.
'All the better to see you with,'
the Wolf replied.

He sat there watching her and smiled.
He thought, I'm going to eat this child.
Compared with her old Grandmamma,
She's going to taste like caviar.

Then Little Red Riding Hood said,
'But Grandma, what a lovely great big
furry coat you have on.'

'That's wrong!' cried Wolf.
'Have you forgot
To tell me what BIG TEETH I've got?
Ah well, no matter what you say,
I'm going to eat you anyway.'
The small girl smiles. One eyelid flickers.
She whips a pistol from her knickers.

She aims it at the creature's head,
And bang bang bang, she shoots him dead.
A few weeks later, in the wood,
I came across Miss Riding Hood.
But what a change! No cloak of red,
No silly hood upon her head.
She said, 'Hello, and do please note
My lovely furry wolfskin coat.'

This poem is another rewriting of a traditional fairy tale,
this time from Goldilocks's perspective.

I'd listened at the door; they were always there,
the daddy with the voice and the enormous chair,
the mummy with the pinny, stirring the vat;
banging his spoon, their spoilt wee brat.

The chance came soon; they were humouring
the kid, swinging him hand to hand,
There there, baby bear, let's leave our bowls,
walk in the forest till the porridge cools.

All the more for me; I walked in from the yard
climbed onto daddy's chair – far too hard.
You know the score – hard, soft, right,
hot, cold, fine; big, small, mine.

Point was I had the whole place to myself,
put telly on, took a bath, rearranged a shelf.
Then it was Who's been sitting in our chairs,
helping themselves? Beds are for bears

and this one's bust. Yeah, yeah, fair cop.
But they chased after me and didn't stop
till jumping out the window was the only way;
and there's me thinking they'd ask me to stay.

But I'll be back, you mark my words;
bears living in houses! It's just absurd;
bears eating porridge, bears wearing frocks –
next time they're out I'm changing the locks.

271

This poem is another re-imagining of a familiar story, and Rachel Rooney uses the understated form of a property advertisement to tell the story of the Three Little Pigs.

> Two houses up for sale.
> One stick, one straw.
> Both self-assembly,
> See pig next door.

24 August · The Rainy Day ·
Henry Wadsworth Longfellow

Unfortunately, summer can't last forever – soon
strawberries and trips to the seaside will be replaced
by falling leaves and chestnuts and that old British
favourite: rain! Longfellow's poem treats the start of
autumn as a mental state, but the narrator's dejection
soon passes as if it were itself a rain shower.

The day is cold, and dark, and dreary;
It rains, and the wind is never weary;
The vine still clings to the mouldering wall,
But at every gust the dead leaves fall,
    And the day is dark and dreary.

My life is cold, and dark, and dreary;
It rains, and the wind is never weary;
My thoughts still cling to the mouldering Past,
But the hopes of youth fall thick in the blast,
    And the days are dark and dreary.

Be still, sad heart! and cease repining;
Behind the clouds is the sun still shining;
Thy fate is the common fate of all,
Into each life some rain must fall,
    Some days must be dark and dreary.

25 August · The Splendour Falls on Castle Walls (*from* The Princess) · Alfred, Lord Tennyson

This song-like poem by Tennyson seems to act out the 'wild echoes' which it describes. The poet conjures up images of a beautiful realm in which the horns of Elfland echo across hills and lakes, growing louder forever. Unsurprisingly, given these horn calls in Tennyson's poem, the composer Benjamin Britten set this to music in his Serenade for Tenor, Horn and Strings.

The splendour falls on castle walls
    And snowy summits old in story:
  The long light shakes across the lakes,
    And the wild cataract leaps in glory.
Blow, bugle, blow, set the wild echoes flying,
Blow, bugle; answer, echoes, dying, dying, dying.

    O hark, O hear! how thin and clear,
    And thinner, clearer, farther going!
  O sweet and far from cliff and scar
    The horns of Elfland faintly blowing!
Blow, let us hear the purple glens replying:
Blow, bugle; answer, echoes, dying, dying, dying.

    O love, they die in yon rich sky,
    They faint on hill or field or river:
  Our echoes roll from soul to soul,
    And grow for ever and for ever.
Blow, bugle, blow, set the wild echoes flying,
And answer, echoes, answer, dying, dying, dying.

25 August · So, We'll Go No More a-Roving · George Gordon, Lord Byron

Byron is known for his often outrageous writings and misadventures – Lady Caroline Lamb called him 'mad, bad, and dangerous to know', a phrase that has been attached to his name ever since.

So, we'll go no more a-roving
  So late into the night,
Though the heart be still as loving,
  And the moon be still as bright.

For the sword outwears its sheath,
  And the soul wears out the breast,
And the heart must pause to breathe,
  And love itself have rest.

Though the night was made for loving,
  And the day returns too soon,
Yet we'll go no more a-roving
  By the light of the moon.

275

26 August · Fear No More the Heat o' the Sun · William Shakespeare

This extract from Shakespeare's *Cymbeline* is actually a burial song, but its words act as a tribute to the passing of the seasons and the movements of the year.

Fear no more the heat o' the sun,
   Nor the furious winter's rages;
Thou thy worldly task hast done,
   Home art gone, and ta'en thy wages.
Golden lads and girls all must,
As chimney-sweepers, come to dust.

Fear no more the frown o' the great;
   Thou art past the tyrant's stroke;
Care no more to clothe and eat,
   To thee the reed is as the oak.
The sceptre, learning, physic, must
All follow this, and come to dust.

Fear no more the lightning-flash,
   Nor the all-dreaded thunder-stone;
Fear not slander, censure rash;
   Thou hast finished joy and moan.
All lovers young, all lovers must
Consign to thee, and come to dust.

No exorcizer harm thee!
Nor no witchcraft charm thee!
Ghost unlaid forbear thee!
Nothing ill come near thee!
Quiet consummation have,
And renownèd be thy grave!

In this poem, Thomas describes meeting the mysterious
bird of the title. Just the memory of the bird's song can
lift his spirits.

Three lovely notes he whistled, too soft to be heard
If others sang; but others never sang
In the great beech-wood all that May and June.
No one saw him: I alone could hear him:
Though many listened. Was it but four years
Ago? or five? He never came again.

Oftenest when I heard him I was alone,
Nor could I ever make another hear.
La-la-la! he called, seeming far-off —As if a cock
crowed past the edge of the world,
As if the bird or I were in a dream.
Yet that he travelled through the trees and sometimes
Neared me, was plain, though somehow distant still
He sounded. All the proof is – I told men
What I had heard.

I never knew a voice,
Man, beast, or bird, better than this. I told
The naturalists; but neither had they heard
Anything like the notes that did so haunt me,
I had them clear by heart and have them still.
Four years, or five, have made no difference. Then
As now that La-la-la! was bodiless sweet:
Sad more than joyful it was, if I must say
That it was one or other, but if sad
'Twas sad only with joy too, too far off
For me to taste it. But I cannot tell
If truly never anything but fair
The days were when he sang, as now they seem.
This surely I know, that I who listened then,
Happy sometimes, sometimes suffering
A heavy body and a heavy heart,
Now straightway, if I think of it, become
Light as that bird wandering beyond my shore.

Mark Haddon is perhaps best known as the novelist
of the celebrated bestseller, *The Curious Incident of
the Dog in the Night-Time*. In this poem he exalts the
unassuming beauty of trees, which, despite being ever-
present and grand in stature, are rarely appreciated.
Here Haddon encourages us to notice these little
natural stories that unfold outside our windows, and
often outside our notice – from roaring oaks to the
emergence of a new generation of trees.

They stand in parks and graveyards and gardens.
Some of them are taller than department stores,
yet they do not draw attention to themselves.

You will be fitting a heated towel rail one day
and see, through the louvre window,
a shoal of olive-green fish changing direction
in the air that swims above the little gardens.

Or you will wake at your aunt's cottage,
your sleep broken by a coal train on the empty hill
as the oaks roar in the wind off the channel.

Your kindness to animals, your skill at the clarinet,
these are accidental things.
We lost this game a long way back.
Look at you. You're reading poetry.
Outside the spring air is thick
with the seeds of their children.

• How to Cut a Pomegranate •
Imtiaz Dharker

In this poem the pomegranate is more than just a fruit.
Its exotic taste transforms it into a symbol of a distant
home, with each seed containing a wealth of flavours,
sounds and sights.

'Never,' said my father,
'Never cut a pomegranate
through the heart. It will weep blood.
Treat it delicately, with respect.

'Just slit the upper skin across four quarters.
This is a magic fruit,
so when you split it open, be prepared
for the jewels of the world to tumble out,
more precious than garnets,
more lustrous than rubies,
lit as if from inside.
Each jewel contains a living seed.
Separate one crystal.
Hold it up to catch the light.
Inside is a whole universe.
No common jewel can give you this.'

Afterwards, I tried to make necklaces
of pomegranate seeds.
The juice spurted out, bright crimson,
and stained my fingers, then my mouth.
I didn't mind. The juice tasted of gardens

I had never seen, voluptuous
with myrtle, lemon, jasmine,
and alive with parrots' wings.

The pomegranate reminded me
that somewhere I had another home.

✹ 28 August · Dawn · Paul Laurence Dunbar

This short stanza by the American poet Paul Laurence
Dunbar takes the moment of sunrise as its subject.

> An angel, robed in spotless white,
> Bent down and kissed the sleeping Night.
> Night woke to blush; the sprite was gone.
> Men saw the blush and called it Dawn.

28 August · *from* The Task · William Cowper

On 28 August 1833, the Slavery Abolition Act was passed in the Houses of Parliament. Though it did not immediately end slavery in British colonies, it was the beginning of its end. Part of the reasoning that inspired the act – beyond the major ethical arguments against all forms of slavery in general – was that slavery was not tolerated in Britain, and therefore should not be tolerated in British colonies. This is an argument expressed many years earlier, in Cowper's epic poem from 1785, *The Task*.

I would not have a slave to till my ground,
To carry me, to fan me while I sleep,
And tremble when I wake, for all the wealth
That sinews bought and sold have ever earn'd.
No: dear as freedom is, and in my heart's
Just estimation priz'd above all price,
I had much rather be myself the slave
And wear the bonds, than fasten them on him.
We have no slaves at home. – Then why abroad?
And they themselves, once ferried o'er the wave
That parts us, are emancipate and loos'd.
Slaves cannot breathe in England; if their lungs
Receive our air, that moment they are free;
They touch our country and their shackles fall.
That's noble, and bespeaks a nation proud
And jealous of the blessing. Spread it then,
And let it circulate through ev'ry vein
Of all your empire; that where Britain's pow'r
Is felt, mankind may feel her mercy too.

✹ 29 August · No More Auction Block · Anon.

The lyrics to the song 'No More Auction Block' date back to the American Civil War, when it was a marching song sung by African-American soldiers. The lyrics reject various aspects of a slave's life and with frequent use of repetition for emphasis, the song broadcasts a powerful message.

No more auction block for me
No more, no more
No more auction block for me
Many thousand gone.

No more peck of corn for me
No more, no more
No more peck of corn for me
Many thousand gone.

No more driver's lash for me
No more, no more
No more driver's lash for me
Many thousand gone.

No more pint of salt for me
No more, no more
No more pint of salt for me
Many thousand gone.

No more hundred lash for me
No more, no more
No more hundred lash for me
Many thousand gone.

No more mistress' call for me
No more, no more
No more mistress' call for me
Many thousand gone.

Prayer can be difficult to describe. Here, the
seventeenth-century poet George Herbert explains what
praying means to him.

Prayer the Church's banquet, angels' age,
    God's breath in man returning to his birth,
    The soul in paraphrase, heart in pilgrimage,
The Christian plummet sounding heav'n and earth;
Engine against th' Almighty, sinners' tow'r,
    Reversed thunder, Christ-side-piercing spear,
    The six-days' world transposing in an hour,
A kind of tune, which all things hear and fear;
Softness, and peace, and joy, and love, and bliss,
    Exalted manna, gladness of the best,
    Heaven in ordinary, man well drest,
The milky way, the bird of Paradise,
    Church-bells beyond the stars heard, the soul's blood,
    The land of spices; something understood.

Bob Dylan is one of the most successful songwriters of the last sixty years, and is especially noted for his many songs on social and political themes. He was awarded the Nobel Prize for Literature in 2016, the first time the prize had been won by a popular musician.

How many roads must a man walk down
Before you call him a man?
Yes, 'n' how many seas must a white dove sail
Before she sleeps in the sand?
Yes, 'n' how many times must the cannonballs fly
Before they're forever banned?
The answer, my friend, is blowin' in the wind
The answer is blowin' in the wind

How many years can a mountain exist
Before it's washed to the sea?
Yes, 'n' how many years can some people exist
Before they're allowed to be free?
Yes, 'n' how many times can a man turn his head
Pretending he just doesn't see?
The answer, my friend, is blowin' in the wind
The answer is blowin' in the wind

How many times must a man look up
Before he can see the sky?
Yes, 'n' how many ears must one man have
Before he can hear people cry?
Yes, 'n' how many deaths will it take till he knows
That too many people have died?
The answer, my friend, is blowin' in the wind
The answer is blowin' in the wind

This poem by C. S. Lewis, perhaps better known as
the author of the *Chronicles of Narnia* books, was
written in 1948, and tells a story based on Noah's Ark.
In Lewis's reimagining, Noah's sons, Shem, Ham and
Japhet, are too lazy to let in the unicorn, meaning the
world will be deprived of these creatures.

The sky was low, the sounding rain was falling dense
    and dark,
And Noah's sons were standing at the window of the Ark.

The beasts were in, but Japhet said, 'I see one creature
    more
Belated and unmated there come knocking at the door.'

'Well, let him knock,' said Ham, 'Or let him drown or
    learn to swim.
We're overcrowded as it is; we've got no room for him.'

'And yet it knocks, how terribly it knocks,' said Shem,
    'Its feet
Are hard as horn – but oh the air that comes from it is
    sweet.'

'Now hush,' said Ham, 'You'll waken Dad, and once he
    comes to see
What's at the door, it's sure to mean more work for you
    and me.'

Noah's voice came roaring from the darkness down below,
'Some animal is knocking. Take it in before we go.'

Ham shouted back, and savagely he nudged the other two,
'That's only Japhet knocking down a brad-nail in his shoe.'

Said Noah, 'Boys, I hear a noise that's like a horse's
    hoof.'
Said Ham, 'Why, that's the dreadful rain that drums
    upon the roof.'
Noah tumbled up on deck and out he put his head;
His face went grey, his knees were loosed, he tore his
    beard and said,

'Look, look! It would not wait. It turns away. It takes its
    flight.
Fine work you've made of it, my sons, between you all
    tonight!

'Even if I could outrun it now, it would not turn again –
Not now. Our great discourtesy has earned its high
    disdain.

'Oh noble and unmated beast, my sons were all unkind;
In such a night what stable and what manger will you
    find?

'Oh golden hoofs, oh cataracts of mane, oh nostrils wide
With indignation! Oh the neck wave-arched, the lovely
    pride!

'Oh long shall be the furrows ploughed across the hearts
    of men
Before it comes to stable and to manger once again.

'And dark and crooked all the ways in which our race
    shall walk,
And shrivelled all their manhood like a flower with
    broken stalk,

'And all the world, oh Ham, may curse the hour when
    you were born;
Because of you the Ark must sail without the Unicorn.'

31 August · The Destruction of Sennacherib · George Gordon, Lord Byron

'The Destruction of Sennacherib' is another poetic retelling of a Biblical tale, although Byron's adaptation of an episode in the second part of the Book of Kings – in which the Israelites are protected from the Assyrian siege of Jerusalem by a ruthless angel – is much more dramatic, and darker, than Lewis's unicorn parable. Like 'Ozymandias' by Byron's Romantic contemporary Percy Bysshe Shelley, the poem serves as a warning that even the most powerful cannot escape their inevitable demise. Here Byron uses the transition of a verdant summer into an autumn of decay as a simile for the collapse of the invading army, making it a fitting read for the last day of August.

The Assyrian came down like the wolf on the fold,
And his cohorts were gleaming in purple and gold;
And the sheen of their spears was like stars on the sea,
When the blue wave rolls nightly on deep Galilee.

Like the leaves of the forest when Summer is green,
That host with their banners at sunset were seen:
Like the leaves of the forest when Autumn hath blown,
That host on the morrow lay wither'd and strown.

For the Angel of Death spread his wings on the blast,
And breathed in the face of the foe as he passed;
And the eyes of the sleepers waxed deadly and chill,
And their hearts but once heaved, and for ever grew still!

And there lay the steed with his nostril all wide,
But through it there rolled not the breath of his pride;
And the foam of his gasping lay white on the turf,
And cold as the spray of the rock-beating surf.

And there lay the rider distorted and pale,
With the dew on his brow, and the rust on his mail:
And the tents were all silent, the banners alone,
The lances unlifted, the trumpet unblown.

And the widows of Ashur are loud in their wail,
And the idols are broke in the temple of Baal;
And the might of the Gentile, unsmote by the sword,
Hath melted like snow in the glance of the Lord!

31 August • Fly Away, Fly Away Over the Sea • Christina Rossetti

In just four lines Christina Rossetti captures the bittersweet mixture of emotions that we encounter on 31 August, when 'summer is done'. On the one hand, we watch the swallows begin their journey south with trepidation about the dark and cold days to come. On the other, their leaving fills us with an eager anticipation of their – and summer's – yearly return.

Fly away, fly away over the sea,
  Sun-loving swallow, for summer is done;
Come again, come again, come back to me,
  Bringing the summer and bringing the sun.

Index of First Lines

295

297

Index of Poets and Translators

299

Acknowledgements

The compiler and publisher would like to thank the following for permission to reproduce copyright material:

Angelou, Maya: 'Harlem Hopscotch' from *Just Give Me a Cool Drink of Water* copyright © Maya Angelou 1988. Reprinted by permission of Virago, an imprint of Little, Brown Book Group; **Ardagh, Philip**: 'Remembered More for His Beard', originally published in *A Poem for Every Day of the Year* edited by Allie Esiri, Macmillan Children's Books, 2017. Used by permission of the author; **Baldwin, James:** 'Imagination' from *Jimmy's Blues and Other Poems* by James Baldwin Copyright © 2013 The James Baldwin Estate. Reprinted by permission of Beacon Press, Boston; **Bentley, E.C:** 'Alfred, Lord Tennyson' and 'Wolfgang Amadeus Mozart' reproduced with permission of Curtis Brown Group Ltd, London, on behalf of The Beneficiary of the Estate of E. C. Bentley © The Beneficiary of the Estate of E. C. Bentley, 2016; **Betjeman, John:** 'Hunter Trials' © The Estate of John Betjeman 1955, 1958, 1960, 1962, 1964, 1966, 1970, 1979, 1981, 1982, 2001. Reproduced by permission of Hodder and Stoughton Limited; **Bilston, Brian:** 'Refugees' from *You Took the Last Bus Home* (Unbound, 2016) copyright © Brian Bilston 2016; **Bromley, Carole:** 'Goldilocks' was shortlisted for the Manchester Writing for Children Award 2015, performed at the CLiPPA Awards and published in *Let in the Stars* (ed. Mandy Coe). Used with permission of author; **Causley, Charles:** 'Song of the Dying Gunner' and 'My Mother Saw a Dancing Bear' from *Collected Poems for Children* (Macmillan Children's Books, 2016), used with permission of David Higham Associates on behalf of the estate of the author; **Coe, Mandy:** 'Amelia Earheart', used with permission of author; **Collins, Billy:** 'On Turning Ten' and 'Walking Across the Atlantic' from *Taking Off Emily Dickinson's Clothes* (Picador, 2000) copyright © Billy Collins. All published by permission of Picador, London; **Cookson, Paul:** 'Father's Hands' copyright © Paul Cookson. First published in *The Very Best of Paul Cookson,* Macmillan Children's Books 2001. Used with permission of the author; **Cope, Wendy:** 'Shakespeare at School' copyright © Wendy Cope 2016. Reproduced by permission of Faber & Faber Ltd; **Cummings, E.E:** 'maggie and milly and molly and may' Copyright © 1956, 1984, 1991 by the Trustees for the E. E. Cummings Trust, "next to of course god america i" Copyright 1926, 1954, © 1991 by the Trustees for the E. E. Cummings Trust. Copyright © 1985 by George James Firmage, from *Complete Poems: 1904-1962* by E. E. Cummings, edited by George J. Firmage. Used by permission of Liveright Publishing Corporation; **Dahl, Roald:** 'The Pig' from *Dirty Beasts* published by Jonathan Cape Ltd & Penguin Books Ltd, 'Little Red Riding Hood and the Wolf' from *Revolting Rhymes* published by Jonathan Cape Ltd & Penguin Books Ltd © The Roald Dahl Story Company Limited. All poems published by permission of David Higham Associates on behalf of the estate of the author; **De la Mare, Walter:** 'Silver' and 'The Listeners' Tartary' copyright © Walter de la Mare. Reprinted by permission of The Literary Trustees of Walter de la Mare and The Society of Authors as their Representative; **Dharker, Imtiaz:** 'How to Cut a Pomegranate' 'How to Cut a Pomegranate' from *The terrorist at my table* (Bloodaxe Books, 2006). Reproduced with permission of Bloodaxe Books; **Doolittle, Hilda:** 'Heat'Copyright © 1982 by the Estate of Hilda Doolittle. Reproduced by permission of Carcanet Press Limited; **Duffy, Carol Ann:** 'Originally' from The Other Country by Carol Ann Duffy. Published by Anvil Press, 1990. Copyright © Carol Ann Duffy. Reproduced by permission of the author c/o Rogers, Coleridge & White Ltd., 20 Powis Mews, London W11 1JN; **Dylan, Bob:** 'Blowin' in the Wind' by Bob Dylan, Words and Music by Bob Dylan © Universal Tunes (SESAC). Reprinted by permission of Universal Music. **Ferlinghetti, Lawrence:** 'Don't Let That Horse . . . (#14)' by Lawrence Ferlinghetti from *A Coney Island of the Mind* copyright © 1958 by Lawrence Ferlinghetti. Reprinted by permission of New Directions Publishing Corp; **Graves, Robert:** 'I'd Love to be a Fairy's Child' from *Fairies and Fusiliers* by Robert Graves (Carcanet Press Limited) and 'The Cruel Moon' from *The Complete Poems in One Volume* by Robert Graves. Printed by permission of Carcanet Press Limited; **Haddon, Mark:** 'Trees' from *The Talking Horse and the Sad Girl and the Village Under the Sea* (Picador, 2005) copyright © Mark Haddon. Used by permission of Picador, London; **Heaney, Seamus:** 'Blackberry-Picking' from *New and Selected Poems 1966– 1987* by Seamus Heaney (Faber and Faber Ltd). All poems published by permission of Faber and Faber Ltd; **Hughes, Langston:** 'To You' and 'If-ing' from *The Collected Poems of Langston Hughes* published by Alfred A. Knopf Inc. All poems published by permission of David Higham Associates on behalf of the estate of the author; **Larkin, Philip:** 'MCMXIV' from *The Complete Poems* by Philip Larkin (Faber and Faber Ltd). All poems published by permission of Faber and Faber Ltd; **Lee, Laurie**: 'Apples' reproduced with permission of Curtis Brown Group Ltd, London, on behalf of The Beneficiaries of the Estate of Laurie Lee copyright © The Partners of the Literary Estate of Laurie Lee, 2016; **Lewis, C.S**: 'The Late Passenger' from Poems. copyright © C.S. Lewis Pte. Ltd. 1964. Reprinted by permission; **Logue, Christopher:** 'Come to the Edge' from *Selected Poems* by Christopher Logue (Faber and Faber Ltd) published by permission of Faber and Faber Ltd; **MacNeice, Louis:** 'Prayer Before Birth' from *Collected Poems* copyright © Louise MacNeice (Faber & Faber, 2016); **McGough, Roger:** 'The Way Things Are' from *The Way Things Are* (Penguin, 2000) copyright © Roger McGough. All poems reprinted by permission of Penguin Random House; **Milligan, Spike:** 'The Land of the Bumbley Boo' from *A Children's Treasury of Milligan* by Spike Milligan (Virgin Books, 2006 and 'Casabianca (A Parody)' copyright © Spike Milligan. All poems published by permission of Spike Milligan Productions Ltd; **Milne, A. A.:** The End' an extract from *Now We Are Six* by A. A. Milne. All text copyright © The Trustees of the Pooh Properties 1924. Published with permission of Curtis Brown Group Ltd; **Morgan, Edwin:**

'Particle Poems' from *Collected Poems* by Edwin Morgan (Carcanet Press Limited, 1990) copyright © Edwin Morgan. Reproduced by permission of Carcanet Press Limited; **Mucha, Laura:** 'The Land of the Blue' and 'Just One' copyright © Laura Mucha. Printed by permission of the author; **Muir, Edwin:** 'The Horses' from *Collected Poems* by EdwinMuir (Faber & Faber Ltd, 1984) copyright © Willa Muir, 1960, 1979. Reproduced by permission of Faber & Faber Ltd; **Nash, Ogden:** 'A Flea and a Fly' from *Candy is Dandy* published by André Deutsch, 1994; **Nesbitt, Kenn:** 'Einstein's Brain' © 2004 Kenn Nesbitt. All Rights Reserved. Reprinted by permission of the author; **Oliver, Mary:** 'The Summer Day' from *House of Light* by Mary Oliver, published by Beacon Press, Boston, copyright © 1990 by Mary Oliver, used herewith by permission of the Charlotte Sheedy Literary Agency, Inc.; **Palmer, Ros:** 'The Puzzles and the Stolen Jewels' by permission of the author; **Plath, Sylvia:** 'Balloons' from *Collected Poems* (Faber & Faber Ltd, 2002). Copyright © The Estate of Sylvia Plath, 1965. Published by permission of Faber & Faber Ltd; **Rice, John:** 'The Fairy School Under the Loch' copyright © John Rice. First published in *Green Glass Beads* ed. Jacqueline Wilson, Macmillan Children's Books 2011; **Roethke, Theodore:** 'The meadow Mouse' and 'Sloth' from *Collected Poems* (Faber & Faber Ltd, 1985) copyright © Theodore Roethke, 1985. Reproduced by permission of Faber & Faber Ltd; **Rooney, Rachel:** 'Property for Sale' by permission of the author; **Sassoon, Siegfried:** 'The Dug-out' copyright © Siegfried Sassoon by kind permission of the Estate of George Sassoon; **Smith, Stevie:** 'The Pleasure of Friendship' and 'The Forlorn Sea' from *Collected Poems and Drawings* by Stevie Smith (Faber and Faber Ltd). All poems published by permission of Faber and Faber Ltd; **St. Vincent Millay, Edna**: 'Travel' copyright © Edna St Vincent Millay. Reproduced by permission of A.M Heath & Co Ltd; **Tempest, Kae:** 'Watching my Dog Sleep' from *Hold Your Own* copyright © Kate Tempest (Picador, 2014). Printed by permission of Picador; **Thomas, Dylan:** 'And Death Shall Have No Dominion' and 'Fern Hill' from *The Collected Poems of Dylan Thomas: The Centenary Edition* copyright © Dylan Thomas (Weidenfeld & Nicolson, 2016). All poems published by permission of David Higham Associates on behalf of the estate of the author; **Updike, John:** 'June' and 'August' from *A Child's Calendar* copyright © John Updike (Holiday House, 2002). Used with permission by the Wylie Agency. **Walcott, Derek:** 'Midsummer, Tobago' from *The Poetry of Derek Walcott* (Faber and Faber). Reproduced by permission of Faber & Faber Ltd; **Watts, Anthony:** 'End of the Day' by kind permission of the author; **Wright, Franz:** Auto-Lullaby from *Walking To Martha's Vineyard* by Franz Wright, copyright © 2003 by Franz Wright. Used by permission of Alfred A. Knopf, an imprint of the Knopf Doubleday Publishing Group, a division of Penguin Random House LLC. All rights reserved.

Every effort has been made to trace the copyright holders, but if any have been inadvertently overlooked the publisher will be pleased to make the necessary arrangement at the first opportunity.